SAFE

SAFE

Jill Case Brown

Interior art by Heidi Likins

Published in USA
ISBN-13:978-1503337701
ISBN-10:1503337707 (Kindle)

TO MY HUSBAND, DAVID
who got me into this in the first place
and
THE BUNNY-CATCHERS
who keep me going:
Mary Davis
Jim Hart
Heidi Likins
Donita K. Paul
Carol Reinsma
Faye Spieker

1

Prickle

I came home charged and chuffed, letting the door bang shut behind me. The car keys felt cold and powerful in my jeans pocket. Today had been my first time to drive to school on my own, and I felt *great*.

"I'm home!"

My size thirteen Nikes thumped against the hardwood floor as I went into the dining room, automatically ducking my head in the doorway. I slung my book bag across the floor toward the stairs. It hit the bottom step with a satisfying *whump*.

"Hey, I'm home!" Peeling off my jacket, I dropped it over the back of a chair. Then I stood still and listened.

Nothing.

Nothing but echoes of the noises I'd just made dying away…and furtive scrabbling sounds from the kitchen.

It could almost have been my imagination. But not quite.

I wouldn't say it scared me, but my arms and head prickled as the hairs popped up from the skin. I hate that. Even if you aren't really scared, that hair-prickle thing makes you think you are. I shook my head, shoved the hair out of my eyes, and yanked down the sleeves of my sweatshirt.

"Okay, manly-man. Let's go." My feet didn't want to move toward the kitchen, but I didn't give them a choice. *Step one, step two, step three*.

I stopped in the doorway and looked around. No one in sight. The refrigerator blocked my view of part of the room, so I leaned out to see around it. My eyes slid reluctantly toward the back door.

That was when I saw her.

Crouching in the corner between the deep freeze and the door, she had her back partly toward me. Her face was turned away, so all I could see was the gleam of dark hair pulled back in a ponytail. A flannel shirttail hung below her thick blue sweater, but her feet were bare. One arm arched over her head, her hand gripping the doorknob so hard I could see the white knuckles and stretched tendons from across the room.

I could also see she wasn't going to get the door open. Not with the deadbolt fastened like that.

"Um, excuse me." I stepped out from behind the refrigerator. "Who're you?"

The crouching figure jerked. Her hand slid off the knob. She twisted to stare up at me and edged deeper into the corner, slow and silent, as if trying to fade into the wall.

I moved back half a step. "Hey, it's okay."

Her eyes looked huge, her face so white it was hard to believe there could be any blood behind the skin.

I smiled and tried to look harmless. "It's just me. Bank."

Finally, her pale lips moved. The words sounded tight, as if somebody had her by the throat, but they carried across the room the way a whisper does. "Are you a boy?"

I nodded. "I'm Bank. Bank Jonsson. I'm a boy."

"You're so big. Are you…safe?"

"I'm really safe." I nodded again. "Just ask Gatekeeper."

Her eyes changed then. I watched them go blank, the big pupils shrinking, the eyelids lowering. Her chin dropped. Color washed into her cheeks and across her forehead.

I waited.

She blinked a couple of times and looked around at the floor, as if puzzled by finding herself squashed into a corner of the kitchen. One finger reached down to touch her bare toes. She frowned. Then her head came up, and she saw me.

"Bank." Her eyes brightened. "You're home."

2

"Hey, Mom." I went over to give her a hand up and smiled down at her. "So. Who was that?"

2

Jeff

After dinner, upstairs in my room, I sat at the computer and waggled the mouse to wake it up. It made little crunching noises. I picked it up and swiped my hand across the mouse pad, then licked my fingers. Cookie crumbs. That might explain why the bottom row of my keyboard was sticking, too.

Oh, well. I reached into my official snack drawer, popped a handful of cheese crackers into my mouth, and brushed a new crop of crumbs off the desk. Then I opened my inbox.

To: bankrobber@cvc.org
From: jeffers@moondog.com
Subject: brrrrrrrrrrrr

I grinned. When we emailed each other, Jeff and I never put anything in the subject line. We just left it blank. If we had nothing to say, though, we stuck in some random subject as a signal to the other person. *Just saying hi, don't bother to open this.*

Lately, Jeff always used *brrrrrrrrrrr*, give or take a few *r*'s. His family had moved to Minnesota during Christmas break, exactly a week and three days ago, and he couldn't get over how cold it was. His first day at school, he claimed he'd stopped outside the front door to shift his book bag to the other shoulder, and it took three kids to break him loose from the sidewalk. *Great way to meet people,* he'd written. *Just freeze in place.*

Shoving in another handful of crackers, I wiped my fingers

4

on my jeans and hit *reply*.

To: jeffers@moondog.com
From: bankrobber@cvc.org
Subject:

Hey Jefferson. How you doing? How's the frozen north? Still frozen I guess. Trish Vespers asked about you, said to say hi. Hi☺

Got your happy 16th. Very funny. You're right, 1/11/05 will go down in history as the day the roads of Oklahoma became unsafe. I got my license first try. Drove myself to school today and only took out 3 cars 2 joggers and a kid on a bike. No problem.

This is sucky though. Dad's making me go to a shrink tomorrow to figure out why I'm so normal when nobody else in the family is. I guess normal is a problem or something.☺ He didn't tell me about it til dinner with Mom right there so I couldn't say anything. Ha! He forgot she's going to some church thing with a friend tonight so I'll get him then. If she actually makes it out the door.

Today when I got home somebody new was out and wouldn't answer. It was just because she didn't know me but it gave me the creeps. Ever since that time

I slumped back in my chair and stared at the last few lines. Then I highlighted them and hit the *delete* key with a sharp click. Jeff had lived next door since before either of us was born, and he'd always been great about my mom. But I didn't want to remind him about that time. I didn't want to remind myself.

Leaning forward again, I typed:

Hey, new word. Chuffed. It's British. Means really happy and up, like when I got home today with the car in one piece.

Later $

I sent the email whooshing off to the frozen north and sat back, satisfied. *Chuffed.* Jeff should like that. He always complained my words were unusable, but this was a good one. I'd already used it a couple of times today.

I like words.

Long words, short words, weird words. Words you never hear anybody use. I even like some of the more expressive slang. Like *sucky*, which makes me think of some disgusting sea creature slithering along the bottom of the ocean, eating dead things.

But no hokey abbreviations. Words deserve to be what they are.

As for smiley faces, Jeff said putting them in emails was a girly thing to do. So I started doing it to bug him and got addicted. Now they made me feel a little better about just writing—or calling, if he ever got a phone again—and not seeing him.

A little better. Not much.

As I scraped out the last few crackers, the doorbell rang. I heard the front door open and shut. Voices drifted up the stairs. Mom's friend must be here.

I pushed my chair back and went over to stand in the doorway. Dad's voice rumbled, followed by a double hoot of high laughter that bounced against the ceiling under my feet. Definitely Mrs. Jennings. I grinned. Mom didn't have many friends, but the ones she had were interesting. I especially liked this one.

6

Once she'd set herself to go somewhere, Mom didn't like to hang around. Before long, the voices morphed into the cadence of people saying good-bye, moving toward the door, on their way out. She must've turned back for a second, because the words "home by nine" came clearly up the stairs. Her voice sounded anxious but not panicky.

She really was going.

I took a deep breath and headed down the hallway. Since I never won, I usually avoided arguments with my dad, or at least put them off as long as possible. But today's dirty trick was just too much. The door had barely shut behind Mom and Mrs. Jennings when I thumped down the last few stairs and said loudly, "Dad, I don't want to go tomorrow."

He stood at the tall, skinny window next to the door, watching them go down the sidewalk. Without turning, he said, "Go where?"

"To see that shrink."

"He isn't a shrink. He's a therapist."

"Okay." In arguments with my dad, the trick was to not let him distract you onto a side issue. "I don't want to go see that therapist."

"I know you don't. You've made that clear ever since I brought it up." He turned away from the window. Still without looking at me, he crossed the room and dropped into his old blue chair, leaned back, and shut his eyes. His legs stretched halfway across the living room rug, a sloping gray bridge ending in enormous sock feet.

I shifted to face him. "I don't need counseling."

"How do you know what you do or don't need?"

Hearing the first stir in his voice, I braced myself. Even with Mom safely out of the house, any expression of anger felt wrong. Forbidden. I wanted to back away from it.

Instead, I made myself go over and sit on the sofa across from him. If I'd stuck my legs out like his, the two sets would've

7

tangled together, so I planted my feet on the floor and leaned forward. Anybody watching us from outside would've thought he looked relaxed and I was the one likely to blow. Body language can fool you.

"I know more about what I need than anybody else," I said.

"You think so." He opened his eyes. Two round blue stones.

The eye contact made things harder, but I pushed ahead. "I *know* so."

"Well, it won't hurt you to give it a try. If it turns out you're right about not needing this, you won't have wasted anything except a little time." He actually smiled. "I'd think you would appreciate the experience, Bank. You've expressed an interest in counseling as a possible profession."

I could tell he was trying harder than usual to stay reasonable and low-key. For some reason, that opened a space for my own anger to flick up, unexpected and hotter than I remembered from any time since I'd been too little to know better. I almost didn't recognize the feeling.

Then a more familiar shot of dread sloshed out and doused it. What if I got mad like that when *she* was around?

I took a deep breath. "Dad, I'm doing fine. I grew up with this. It doesn't even seem weird to me. It's just normal life."

"I know." He pushed a hand through his hair. "That's what bothers me."

3

Tara

"Dude." Kevin Miller jabbed me in the side. "Who's *that*?"

I shoved his elbow away and started to tell him to keep his sharp appendages to himself. But at the expression on his face, I looked up. "Wow, I don't know. I've never seen her before."

The girl was just coming out of the main office. She stopped to study a paper in her hand. The Bee—Mrs. Benderbee, North High's small-but-mighty principal—came buzzing out and looked at it, too, standing on her toes to see. She pointed toward the stairs.

As the girl looked up and nodded, shiny black hair swung back from my favorite kind of face. Wide at the forehead, with plenty of room for big, far-apart eyes and high cheekbones, then curving in to a small, almost pointy chin, like a little girl's. From here, I couldn't tell what color her eyes were. But it didn't matter. Whatever, she was hot.

No. More than that. She was *pulchritudinous*.

"Wow," I said again.

Kevin laughed. "Must be new. Hey, we could offer to show her around."

"Yeah, right." As if we would. As if she'd want us to.

I hadn't even realized what we were doing, but as we walked down the hall we must have changed angles, homing in on the girl like a couple of paper clips swerving toward a magnet. If we kept going, we would crash right into her. I straightened us out, bumping Kevin to edge him toward the middle of the hall.

She glanced up as we passed and caught me staring at her.

9

Blue eyes. Or were they green? Whatever, she *was* pulchritudinous.

Familiar, too. I frowned. Who did she remind me of?

"Dude!" Kevin elbowed me again. "What was that about? You gave that girl the *ugliest* face." He made an exaggerated scowl, pulling his mouth into a sour horseshoe.

"Oh, shut it. I didn't look like that."

"You *did*, man."

Rob Henders caught up with us, and Kevin started right in. "Dude! This hot new girl looked at Bank here, and he just—"

"You mean that girl in the office? Dark hair, great legs?"

We both nodded.

"Yeah, well." Rob grinned. "I just happened to go in the office myself this morning. Had to talk to The Bee. I was there when she came in."

Trust Rob. Always in the right place, and if not, he got himself there pronto. It was like a gift. He somehow knew where anything interesting was happening, or about to. "Her name's Tara Prentiss," he said. "She's a sophomore—"

Kevin and I slapped hands.

"—and she just moved here from Minneapolis."

"Minneapolis?" My hand dropped. "Hey, that's where Jeff is."

"What's that TV show? Trading Spaces?" Kevin grinned. "Woo-hoo. We got the best of *that* deal. Minneapolis can have Jeff."

I laughed, even though I didn't think it was funny. Having Jeff move away felt more like losing a brother than a friend, with a lifetime of history together. No girl could take his place. Not even a hot one like Tara Prentiss.

"So," I said. "What classes does she have?"

I meant it as a joke, but Rob didn't even hesitate. He actually had them memorized, what subject which hour, everything. It was amazing. Both he and Kevin had several classes with her, but I didn't have any. Kind of unusual. Our school wasn't that big.

"Too bad, V.J." Kevin, small, dark and skinny, called my dad "the Viking"—though not to his face—because Dad's so tall and broad-shouldered and obviously Scandinavian. His name is Erik Jonsson, no joke. That made me Viking Junior, or V.J. "You'll have to leave it to somebody else to rape and pillage this time."

I laughed again, but I didn't think that was funny either. "Well, see you guys later," I said. "Gotta go." I peeled off toward first-hour Spanish.

In the hallway by my class, a scrawny little freshman must've dropped a book. Two bigger guys kicked it around the hall while he squeaked, "Hey, that's mine. Hey, give it here." As the book slid by, I scooped it up and handed it to him. The other guys jeered at me, but I ignored them. As long as I didn't speak and just kept moving, I could mostly stay invisible.

Later, in the computer lab, I checked my email and found two from Jeff.

To: bankrobber@cvc.org
From: jeffers@moondog.com
Subject:

Jeff had left the subject line blank, which meant he'd actually written something. I opened it.

Everybody expects me to wear cowboy boots and say ain't. Maybe I'll try it. You ought to send me the words from that old musical the school put on last semester, and I'll sing it for talent night. You know, O-o-o-oklahoma, where the wind comes something down the plain.

Better hurry, cause talent night's tonight.

J.

I didn't open the second message. I didn't have to. It was complete in itself.

To: bankrobber@cvc.org
From: jeffers@moondog.com
Subject: Miss you, bro

After school, I drove to my appointment with the shrink.

I stopped on the way for four Sonic cheeseburgers and a Dr Pepper, but ate fast because I started worrying about finding the place. My sense of direction stinks, and I hadn't been driving long enough to know my way around some parts of town. This guy wasn't close to school or our house, and I wondered how Dad had picked him. Probably the only shrink on our insurance.

His name was Dr. Kind, no joke. Sounded like a character in a book for kids, along with Mr. Brave the fireman and Mrs. Smart the teacher.

I got the directions out of my wallet and read through them again.

Even with a couple of wrong turns, I got there ten minutes early. I pulled into a parking spot, backed and straightened a couple of times, and turned the engine off. Then I checked in the rearview mirror for leftover cheeseburger. Good thing, too. I peeled a blob of congealed cheese off my chin and ate it.

Then I sat in the car, sucking on a breath mint.

Dr. Kind's office was in the J.D. Dorst Memorial Building, named for a guy who must've done something great and then died. I've never considered it a good idea to name a medical building after a dead person—not the greatest advertising—but at least these offices had to do with mental health, not physical. Besides, he probably left the money in his will to build it. They had to name it after him.

"Cripes, J.D.," I said aloud. "If I was you, I'd come back and haunt them."

A one-story brick rectangle with the name chiseled into a concrete slab above the front door, this building would never win awards for architectural creativity. Flat roof, everything at ninety-degree angles, metal doors spaced evenly along the side. No windows. The place looked like a prison. Appropriate, considering I was here against my will.

Thanks a lot, Dad.

I crunched the last of my breath mint. Okay, so this wasn't a prison, and I hadn't done anything wrong. What if I just didn't go in? Dr. Kind could relax for an hour. Take a nap, have a cup of coffee, read a few articles in whatever magazine shrinks read.

Or he could call Dad and tell him I never showed.

I pulled the keys out of the ignition and shoved the car door open. Knowing my dad, he'd make me pay for whatever a no-show cost. Besides, much as I hated to admit it, he was right.

I *was* curious. I'd never had my head shrunk before.

4

Shrinking

The door into the waiting room opened. When I looked up, my hand jerked and sent *Modern Psychology* sliding off my knee. I grabbed at it but missed.

Dad? Coming out of the shrink's inner sanctum?

No, not my dad, though it took a good long stare to make sure. Just another tall, blond, Viking type, wearing a tweed jacket and tan pants that could've come straight out of my parents' closet. Even the shoes looked familiar.

Before I could recover from the shock of that first impression, he walked up to my chair and stuck out his hand, saying, "You must be Bancroft."

The voice sounded casual, but the eyes obviously weren't missing a thing.

"It's Bank." I scooped the magazine off the floor.

I could tell I sounded more hostile than I'd meant. After all, it wasn't Dr. Kind's fault I'd been stuck with such a wimpy name. It also wasn't his fault he reminded me of the person who *had* stuck me with that name and was making me go to this appointment.

So I stood up and shook hands like a civilized person. I gave him a firm, confident grip, but not so firm and confident it looked like I was trying to prove anything. He must've been at least Dad's height, maybe half an inch taller, so I had to look up to meet his eyes. I wasn't used to that with most people.

"You must be Dr. Kind," I said.

"Actually, it rhymes with pinned." Releasing my hand, he

14

stepped back. "Like the first syllable of kindergarten. Kind."

So. Now we were even.

Once inside his inner sanctum, I glanced around. Not much to see. A desk sat on one side of the room under a painting of two worried-looking cows staring at a tree. Lined up against the opposite wall, three mismatched chairs looked like they were facing a firing squad, with a clock above them counting down the seconds. No other furniture. Two doors, no windows. The walls were blank except for the cows, the clock, and the usual black-framed certificates that proved Dr. Kind was who he said he was and could legally do what he was doing.

I edged closer to his diploma. Erik Jorgensen Kind, no joke. He even had Dad's first name. Feeling as uneasy as the cows, I waited to see what came next.

First, Dr. Kind asked a couple of non-threatening questions. Any trouble finding the place? Would I like something to drink? No to the first, which was basically true. Yes to the second. Then he asked me to turn off my phone.

"There's a wall clock. It's behind you, but if you put your chair right there—" he pointed at a worn place on the beige carpet, "—you can see the clock's reflection in the glass of that picture over the desk. You just have to read it backwards."

Interesting. Had he planned it that way? Probably he'd just noticed his clients watching the cows.

"Go ahead and choose a chair." He opened the door opposite the one we'd come through. "I'll get your Dr Pepper."

Choose a chair. I turned to look at the lineup. This might be a psychological test that would tell him all kinds of weird things about me. Or it might just mean he wanted me to be comfortable. Of the three chairs, I picked the one that should work best with the length of my legs. Setting it on the worn spot, I tested it out.

Not bad. And he was right about the clock.

Dr. Kind came in, shutting the door behind him, and handed me a bottle. "Do you want a cup? Ice?"

15

"No thanks."

"Would you mind if I recorded this session?"

"Sure. I mean, no problem."

He nodded and poked a flat black device on his desk. Then he rolled his own chair out from behind the desk, sat down, and turned to face me at an angle. Not too much of an angle, which might make it seem he wasn't really listening. But not too straight-on, which might seem threatening.

So far, I had a feeling I was putting way more energy into shrinking him than he was me.

"All right, Bank," he said. "Why are you here?"

"My dad. He wanted me to come."

"Why is that?"

His chair creaked as he shifted. At least that made one minor difference from my dad. Anything in our house that creaked or squeaked got an immediate shot of WD-40.

"My mom. She has DID. Dissociative Identity Disorder."

I couldn't tell if he already knew, or if the neutral-but-receptive expression was part of his training. NBR. Maybe he'd even been graded on it. *Your NBR needs work. Never let the client know what's going on in your head.*

"How do you feel about that?" he asked.

"Being here? Or the DID?"

"Either one. Both. Whatever you'd like to talk about. Your appointment is for fifty minutes, and we have forty-one left. They belong to you."

I stared at him. I guess I'd expected a little more structure.

His chair creaked again as he settled back, totally NBR. "Just tell me what you think I should know."

To: jeffers@moondog.com
From: bankrobber@cvc.org
Subject:

Hey Jefferson. None of my ball caps fit anymore. I got my head shrunk today.☺

Dr Kind (rhymes with wind, the kind that O-o-o-oklahoma comes sweepin' down the plain) was okay. He told me to just talk and that's what I did. I went on and on and he just listened. I told him about Mom and lectured him about DID like he didn't already know all about it. Used to be called Multiple Personality Disorder, blah blah blah. He just listened. Then our time was up and he said he looked forward to seeing me next week. Yeah right.

Later $

Hey, new word. Pontificate. It means talk like a know-it-all, the way I did to Dr K.

You wouldn't believe how much Dr K looks like my dad. Viking Clone.

Miss you too bro.

That night, I dreamed about Mom's foster parents. I'd never met them, never even seen a picture of them, but I knew exactly what they looked like.

Evil.

The kind of man who did ugly things to a little girl he'd promised to take care of. And the kind of woman who pretended not to know what was going on. Who called the little girl a liar and slapped her when she tried to tell.

In my dream, I watched people coming to life inside different parts of Mom's brain. *The alters.* Her brain divided up the ugliness and gave it to them.

Choke, Truth, Libby, Killer. Some alters I didn't recognize. But each had a piece of the ugliness to carry.

Some were crying. The pieces they carried had dark spikes that made their hands bleed. Some stood tall. Others crouched. A few wore masks with no expression, and I knew they hid the abuse from the rest of the world. One was laughing, like all the birds in the world singing together, and her hands were empty.

That puzzled me. Then I realized the piece she carried was the biggest of all, but nobody could see it. She hid the worst of the ugliness from the little girl herself.

That was dissociation.

That was how Mom had survived what she called *the ugly years*.

5

Noodle

Thursday morning, I realized Tara Prentiss had Jeff's old locker.

First I felt a jab of resentment. After that, the usual gloom dribbled in. Then I found myself thinking, *Wow, she's gorgeous.* Tara carried herself like a supermodel, graceful and confident. I couldn't figure out why I'd had that sense of familiarity when I first saw her. I didn't exactly hang out with beauty queens.

While I popped a couple of breath mints and changed out my books, I watched Tara messing with her lock, trying to get it open.

Our school building dated back to the 1950s, and bond issues to upgrade it almost never passed. We still had the old, dented lockers that used combination padlocks. That wouldn't be so bad, but the locks the school office handed out must have been even older than the school. To save time and hassle, a lot of kids just set them to look like they were fastened without actually snapping them shut. Which explained the high rate of stuff getting trashed or stolen.

Plus, The Bee was big on random security checks. If she caught your lock undone, she'd take it off, turn it around, and snap it shut with the dial side jammed against the locker. Brutal. You practically had to saw it off to get back in.

Tara made the last spin and jerked her lock several times. Nothing. She muttered, spun it hard, and started in again.

What she needed was WD-40. Dad got me onto that when I was a freshman and had a lock dating back to at least the Civil War. A few squirts of oil, let it sink down deep into the workings of your lock, wipe off the extra, and you were smooth as ice. Maybe I should keep a can of WD-40 in my locker, so I could play hero to any damsel in distress. Then I could take it to my next shrink appointment and take care of Viking Clone's chair.

Grinning, I dug in the bottom of my locker for my Spanish book. Not a bad idea, actually. I could bring the can tomorrow and let Tara—

"Can't get it open?"

I looked over. Alex White stood behind Tara, one hand propped on the next locker so he had her partly boxed in. For a blink of time, the sense of familiarity came back. Another blink, and she was laughing, shoulders straight and self-assured, her big blue—or maybe green—eyes flirting up at him.

She flicked the lock with her fingers. "Either they gave me the wrong combination, or I'm just bein' stupid." The words came out in a slight drawl. "It's so stinkin' *stiff*. It drags and then jumps too far when I try to turn it."

"All these locks are junk. What's your combination?"

She hesitated. Then she turned her hand palm-up and read the numbers off her wrist as Alex worked the lock. I went back to digging in my locker. Funny, the way girls wrote things they wanted to remember on their hands and arms. What happened if you forgot and washed?

Alex got it on the second try.

"*Thanks.* Tomorrow I'll bring my own lock." She pulled a couple of books out and stuffed them into a neon pink book bag. "I've got one that works."

"Better not. They want to be able to get into all the lockers. If they check and you've got a different combination, you're in big trouble. It's like a worse crime than killing somebody."

"I'll *tell* them my new combination."

"And they'll tell you to put the school lock back on." He picked up her book bag. "Just take it home tonight and put some oil on it."

I snapped my lock and spun it the usual half turn. I should've known I wasn't the only one in on the WD-40 fix. Alex's mom worked with my dad, and it sounded like they'd traded tips on their kids' locker problems. You'd think they could find something more interesting to talk about.

Turning away, I heaved my book bag onto my shoulder. If only I wasn't such a coward around girls like Tara, I could be the one standing there. Holding her bag, giving her advice, while she smiled up at me from under those amazing eyelashes. I would actually know what color her eyes were.

"What kind of oil?"

I glanced over again. I liked that little bit of the South in her voice. Minneapolis must not be her hometown.

"Any kind. WD-40, engine oil, even cooking oil. Probably not bath oil." He looked smug when she laughed, which was way more than his pathetic shot at humor deserved. "Drip it down inside and let it sit overnight. It'll work great."

Just before I turned away to head for class, Tara looked up and caught me staring at her. Again.

This time, she was the one to frown.

Mom was in the kitchen when I got home, but today she answered when I called out. As I headed that direction, I heard the oven door shut, and a fantastic smell drifted into the hall. My stomach rumbled.

I was always hungry. I'd been hungry ever since I hit twelve years old and six feet tall, no matter how much I stuffed into myself. Dad joked about getting a second job just to pay for what I ate, and Grandma Jonsson said it served him right. She still liked to tell about the day he came home early from high school and ate everything she'd fixed for the whole family's dinner. Since Dad had three sisters and a brother, that made for a lot of food.

I'd bet I could do that, too. Right now.

"Hey, Mom." I went into the kitchen and slid her a quick look. Then I checked out the pan she'd just taken from the oven. "Is this for dinner?"

"It's for now." She opened a cabinet door. "Apple cake. Sit down and I'll bring you a piece. Ice cream?"

"You know it."

Her sketchbook lay open on the kitchen table. I sat down and leafed through the pages I hadn't seen yet. Sometimes she drew from life, but mostly her sketches came from the fantastic world going on inside her. The more going on inside, the more she drew.

She'd been drawing a lot lately.

They were good, too. She would've been great at fantasy illustrations. But she never let anyone except me see her drawings. And the one time I'd pushed her on the idea of marketing them, I lost my viewing privileges for a few weeks.

The sketchbook slid away from in front of me. A bowl heaped with homemade apple cake and vanilla ice cream clinked down in its place.

"Wow." I plucked out the spoon. "That looks great. Thanks."

She sat down across from me, studied my face, and gave me a tentative smile. "How was your day, Bank?"

My mom, Meredith, was a great listener. The other alters were mostly too scared or too young to get their minds off their own issues, so she always tried to be out when I got home. Tuesday's episode in the kitchen had made for a double exception—not just a different alter, but one I'd never met before. The last time that had happened was when Mom changed shrinks, and Fighter, a tough little five-year-old, came out ready to beat up anybody who tried to get the others to talk.

If Viking Clone found *me* a challenge, he should try my mom.

While I ate two huge pieces of cake, packed with cinnamon

22

and chunks of apple and loaded with vanilla ice cream, I talked about the parts of my day I thought she'd like to hear. Then, for some reason, I told her about Tara.

She smiled. "Do you like her?"

"I don't even know her. I don't know what she's like." I dug my spoon in deep. "All I know is she's way too pretty to be interested in me."

"Bank, you're a good-looking boy."

I snorted. "You *have* to think that. You're my mom. I think I look like a freak."

Her eyes went blank.

"Mom? Um, Meredith?"

She smiled uncertainly, her expression not quite focused. Her left hand moved restlessly on the table. Somebody else was stirring inside, pushing to come out.

Way to go, klutz. I'd forgotten *freak* was one of the words that acted as a trigger, setting off memories from the ugly years. But at least she didn't seem scared, which meant things should be safe enough. I could hang around and see who and what I'd brought out, but I didn't feel like it. This hadn't exactly been a great day.

I scraped up my last spoonful. "Guess I'll go upstairs. I've got a ton of homework." I stood and picked up my bowl. "Thanks, Mom. This was good."

She didn't look up as I left.

In my room, I opened my snack drawer and checked supplies. Getting low. At the back of the drawer, in a crumple of plastic, I found a few Fig Newtons I'd forgotten about. I pried one out and bit into it. A little stale, but not bad.

Stuffing it into my mouth, I turned to the computer. Nothing new from Jeff. I typed:

To: jeffers@moondog.com
From: bankrobber@cvc.org
Subject:

Hey Jefferson. Today at school I tripped over my own gargantuan feet and fell down the stairs. At least I didn't take anyone else down with me. Remember those old horror movies where some normal person gets in the way of an out of control science experiment and swells up into a monster? That's me. A gigantic cooked noodle flapping through the halls of North High while people run screaming out of my way.

Aaaaargh!

Later $

I hit *send* and slumped back in my chair.

No smiley faces in this email. Just remembering myself crashing down the stairs this afternoon, with everybody jumping out of the way or turning to stare and hoot, made me want to move to Minnesota and then keep going. Alaska. Maybe Siberia. I hoped writing Jeff a jokey note about it would give me a little power over the memory. Psychology. I'd have to ask Dr. Kind what he thought of that strategy.

Falling down the stairs had been one part of the day I hadn't told Mom. Things that embarrassed or hurt me scared her, so I tried to edit those out.

Some days, that didn't leave much to tell.

6

Lovejoy

Friday. Basketball game tonight.

Cheerleaders strutted through the halls and classrooms in white jerseys and short red skirts, pretending not to be hyper-aware of how cute and cool they were.

The players wore suits and ties, an old-fashioned tradition I kind of liked. Beneath the formal clothes, they carried an extra energy you could almost see building up through the day, ready to explode onto the court.

A year earlier, Coach Braun had pushed me to try out for the freshman team. I'd asked him to let me think about it. I was tall, sure, but I wasn't coordinated, and I'd never had much interest in sports. No killer instinct. Finally he came and watched while we played basketball in P.E., and I guess that told him what he needed to know. He never said anything else about it.

Now, leaning against the wall before third-hour math while I waited for Rob and Kevin, I tried to imagine if things had gone differently. If I *was* in the game tonight.

One problem, though. My brain had a firm grip on reality and wouldn't play what-if. It knew there was no way I'd get myself out there in front of the whole school with everybody staring, just waiting for me to make an idiot of myself. Falling down, fouling out. Missing the easy point that would've won the game.

No way. I liked to keep myself low-key and out of sight. As much as a six-foot-four-inch cooked noodle could, anyway.

For just a second, though, I got a rush of excitement—

25

"What're you *doing*, dude?"

My eyes snapped open. I hadn't even realized I'd shut them.

Kevin dropped his book bag on the floor next to me and slouched against the wall. "You asleep? Here." He handed me a stick of gum. "Hey, V.J., want to pick me and Rob up for the game tonight? You're the big driver now."

"You know I can't, Kev." The gum was half unwrapped and fuzzy with pocket lint. I handed it back. "Not for six months."

He shrugged. "Who's to know?"

"My dad."

He rolled his eyes. "What? You gonna tell him or something?"

That was another thing I missed about Jeff. Guys would push you into something you didn't want to do, then make you look like a wimp if you said no. Jeff didn't do that. Not to me, at least.

Between Oklahoma law and my dad, if I got caught with more than one underage passenger in the car before my six months was up, I'd get slammed. Probably lose my license. But Kevin didn't care about that. He just wanted a ride, and too bad if it meant trouble for me. If Jeff was here, he'd get after him for that and save me from feeling like an idiot.

A flick of anger shot up, like the other night with my dad.

"Rob's going to make us late. Let's go in." I swung my book bag up so fast it slammed into a girl walking by and knocked her flat.

I couldn't believe it.

She hit the floor facedown, while her book bag went shooting down the hall with everything spilling out. If I could've gone to Siberia that instant, to stay the rest of my life, I would have.

"Dude!" said Kevin. Big help, as usual.

I crouched beside the girl. "Are you okay? Look, I'm really sorry."

She pushed herself up on her elbows and twisted to face me. At first, I thought she was crying. Then I realized she was *laughing*.

26

Concussion. Must be concussion. Maybe she was in shock, hysterical.

She shook her head. "If it's going to happen, it'll happen to me." She rolled over and sat up. "Right, Mandy?"

Then she just sat there in the middle of the hall and laughed, while her friend Mandy collected the books and papers other kids were kicking all over the place. Rob, who must've shown up right after it happened, joined in the cleanup. Kevin leaned against the wall and watched, grinning. I stayed next to the girl on the floor and tried to keep her from getting trampled.

Finally, she let me help her up so we could get out of the way. She stood against the wall, brushing off her jeans and shirt, then ran her fingers through short, curly brown hair.

"I know who you are," she said. Her lips were curly, too, especially when she smiled. "You're Bank Jonsson. We've got biology together."

I nodded. Now I knew who she was. The only person at North High with a worse name than mine.

"You're Lovejoy," I said. "I don't know your last name, though."

"Fox. It's Quaker. So's my first name. We're not Quakers now, but the name Lovejoy goes back in my family forever. I'm the first girl born this generation, so I got the name."

"I'm sorry."

"Why?" She smiled up at me, and the curly dents in the corners of her mouth deepened. Her eyes were a dark, sparkly brown. "I like it. It's different."

"Oh. Sorry."

I should've known. I'd seen Lovejoy coming out of the art room before, and last year she'd won a prize in the city art fair. Best painting, freshman division. Something like that. I'd also seen her wearing an old duffle coat, probably from Army Surplus, that no normal girl would be caught dead in. Arty kids liked to be different. To stand out.

Not me. And in about—I glanced at the hall clock—one more minute, we would all be late to class, one of my least favorite ways to stand out. Maybe Lovejoy didn't care, but I did. I looked up and saw Rob headed our way, carrying her book bag and talking to Mandy.

"You sure you're okay?" I asked, already pushing away from the wall. "I really am sorry."

"Don't worry about it. I'm terrific. We better get going, though." She took the bag from Rob. "Thanks a lot. See you."

She and Mandy took off down the hall. I thought Lovejoy limped a little, but she was moving pretty fast and talking to her friend like nothing was wrong. I saw her head tip back and caught the edge of her laugh. Amazing. I couldn't have picked a nicer person to knock down.

"Way to go, dude." Kevin poked me with his elbow. "What a klutz."

"Oh, shut it." Lately, it seemed like all my so-called conversations with Kevin ended that way. Pushing past him into the classroom, I slumped into my desk.

The giant cooked noodle strikes again.

To: bankrobber@cvc.org
From: jeffers@moondog.com
Subject:

Talent night was a weird mix. I thought these big city kids were supposed to be so sophisticated, but some of it was pretty bad. One guy did a mime act and the only good thing I can say is it was quiet.

The girl who won dressed up like the 60s, love beads and all, and sang an old antiwar song about where all the flowers went. It should have been cheesy but she was good. I mean really good. We have 2 classes together, and she's so quiet you'd never guess she could get up on stage and sing like that. I was ready to go chain myself to the White House fence and protest the war. Any war.

J.

Grinning, I dug into my snack drawer for the last of the fig cookies. I had a feeling I'd hear more about this girl.

I hit *reply*.

To: jeffers@moondog.com
From: bankrobber@cvc.org
Subject:

Hey Jefferson. What's her name? If you want to meet her just knock her down with your book bag. Great way to get a girl's attention.☺ That's what I did to Lovejoy Fox today. The art girl, remember her? She was great about it, but between that and falling down the stairs yesterday I'm ready to move to Minneapolis. Think your parents would adopt me? ☺

Got to go. Basketball game tonight. Rob said Mac would drive Kevin and me, but Kevin's starting to bug me with all this dude dude dude stuff all the time. He's ok but I could use some space right now.

Later $

After that, I called Rob to tell him I'd decided to drive myself.

"You sure? We can swing by. Mac's planning on it."

It *would* be nice to have Rob's brother drop us off at the door. If I drove, I'd probably have to park a mile from the gym, which meant a long hike in the cold. But I was already getting hooked on the freedom of having my own car. I could get away if I needed to.

"No, that's okay," I said. "I'll just meet you guys there."

I pulled on my heavy jacket and snagged my car keys. *Get away if I needed to.* Why had that jumped into my head? As if I'd ever needed to get away from a basketball game.

Shoving the keys into my pocket, I headed for the stairs.

7

Games

As I pulled into a parking spot at the far end of the gym lot, chipmunks started singing "Rudolph the Red-Nosed Reindeer" in my jeans pocket. I braked with a jerk and dug for my phone. The chipmunks got louder. Obnoxious, but Jeff had set the ring tone as a joke just before he moved. I figured I'd hang onto it for a while longer.

I glanced at the number, then flipped it open. "Hey, Rob."

"You here?"

"Yeah." I cut the Prizm's engine. "Where're you?"

"Mac just dropped us off at the door. We're going in."

"I'll find you," I said, just as his end of the connection disintegrated into the roar of an erupting volcano. I yanked the phone away before my eardrums blew out.

No, not a volcano. Way too loud to be anything but the North High gym on game night.

After my long, cold jog across the parking lot, the mass of body heat inside the gym thawed me instantly. I pushed through the yelling, laughing, chomping, glugging, spilling crowd around the concession stand and stopped in the wide doorway to the basketball court. Pulling off my jacket, I scanned the bleachers on the far side for Rob and Kevin.

It took a while to find them. They had seats off to my right, just a couple of rows up. I frowned. What were they doing there? We always sat mid-court on the highest row, and our usual spot was wide open and waiting for us.

I worked my way along the floor in front of the bleachers, trying not to fall over anybody's feet while keeping one eye on the players' warm-up routines. Watching a tall, skinny guy on the opposing team dribble up and sink a perfect shot—*swish!*—I got that same rush of excitement from earlier in the day. Maybe I *could* do that.

The toe of my Nike stubbed against the floor. I lurched a few steps before catching my balance.

"Way to go, flagpole," somebody yelled.

Or maybe I couldn't.

"Come on, let's move up," I said, when I finally got to Rob and Kevin. "I don't like being down this far. You can't see."

"No, this is good." Rob jumped up. "Hey, I'm going to get a Coke. Anybody want anything?"

I sat down and stared after him. We never bought anything at the games. Not since Jeff worked the concession stand and told us the disgusting things kids did to the food and drink before it made it into the hands of the unsuspecting public. According to him, the health department should shut down the concession stand and arrest everybody who'd ever worked there.

"Dude." Kevin's sharp elbow was back in action. "There's that hot new girl. What's her name? Terry?"

"Tara."

"What?"

"Tara," I said, just as he jabbed me again. The word came out louder than I intended. "Hey, Kev, don't *do* that."

I turned to scowl at him. And there she was, right in front of us, gazing at me with startled eyes.

Her eyes...

Her eyes were an amazing blue-green. Just like those pictures of ocean waves with the light coming through the crest where they're about to break. And she had on a sweater exactly the same color. Fuzzy. Soft-looking. By the time I realized I was drowning with my mouth wide open and came up for air, she'd moved on past.

32

Alex White followed her, staring at me as if I really had morphed into the creepy monster noodle from the science experiment.

Great. Way to go, Bank.

I sure wasn't the only guy watching her. Probably every person in those bleachers tracked Tara Prentiss as she walked along the sidelines. She had an incredible figure in tight jeans and that fuzzy sweater, with a leather jacket slung over one shoulder exactly the way a supermodel would carry it. Her black hair sparkled under the bright gym lights. The girl in front of her, a pretty junior named Lisa who dated one of the basketball players, looked chunky and dull in comparison.

No, I wasn't the only guy watching Tara Prentiss. Just the only one who got caught.

Tara had come with a mixed group of guys and girls, a group I liked and wouldn't have minded being part of myself. Smart kids like Alex who didn't seem to care about not being popular, who actually had lives of their own and hung out with people from different years and social backgrounds. I'd seen Lovejoy with them a few times. Some hung out as couples, but not all, and they were the group most likely to be friendly to somebody new. Like Tara.

She probably wouldn't stay with them long, though. The hyper-populars would snap her up in no time.

When she climbed the bleachers at the far end of the gym, disappearing into the crowd, I looked away. In the back of my mind, something about Tara kept poking at me like my own in-brain version of Kevin's elbow. Before I could give it much attention, though, my eyes refocused with a jolt. "Oh, cripes."

"What? What's the matter?" Kevin turned to look. He grinned.

I could've punched him.

Here came Rob with a cardboard tray of drinks, just ahead of Lovejoy and Mandy. And Lovejoy had crutches and a gigantic leg brace.

I couldn't believe it.

Where could I go that was farther away than Siberia?

By the time they got halfway around the court, I'd figured out I would be in debt for the rest of my life, paying off Lovejoy's medical bills. I hadn't told Dad about knocking her down, which meant I'd be grounded for the rest of my life for deceitfulness, or whatever he decided to call it. And if she was permanently disabled, I would hate myself for the rest of my life.

My future didn't look good.

Lovejoy stopped when she saw me, and a strange expression crossed her face. Rob must not have told her I was here. She probably hated me. Her parents were planning to sue me, and she wasn't supposed to talk to me. As if she'd *want* to talk to me.

I looked away so she could pretend she hadn't seen me. "Shut it, Kev."

"What? I didn't say anything."

"You were going to."

He huffed. "Well, I like *that*—"

"Hey, I got you guys Cokes." Rob plunked down onto the bleacher beside me and pulled a cup out of the tray. "Dr Pepper for you, V.J. Everything else is a Coke."

"Thanks." I took it.

He leaned across me to give one to Kevin. When I could see again, Lovejoy and Mandy were settling themselves in front of us. Lovejoy leaned awkwardly down to push her crutches under the bleacher.

Oh, great. This was going to be a really fun game. I might as well go home right now.

Lovejoy twisted around to look up at me. "Bank—"

Rob handed her a Coke. "Here's yours. Sure you don't want one, Mandy?"

"No thanks. Carbonated drinks give me hives."

"That's a new one." He grinned. "I'd like to see that."

"No, you wouldn't. They also make me *mean*." She did a fake roar, curling her fingers into claws.

34

Rob held up the empty drink holder like a shield and pretended to whip at her with the cup in his other hand, like a lion tamer in one of those hokey old circus acts. I stared at him. I'd never seen Rob act that goofy. Either I was crazy, or he was interested in Mandy.

Mandy giggled and clawed at his knee. Wow. It looked like she was interested in him, too. And neither one was being exactly mature about it.

I looked at Kevin.

"Dude," he mumbled. For once, he made sense.

Lovejoy didn't look at me again. I knew I should ask about her leg, even though that was the last thing I wanted to do. I kept thinking she'd turn around, and I'd say something then. But she didn't. Then the game started and the noise level shot up even more, so I would've had to yell for her to hear me. From the start, it was a more exciting game than usual. The aggressive turnovers and dramatic long shots actually pulled me out of my misery now and then.

Lovejoy didn't seem to enjoy it, though. I wondered if her leg hurt a lot.

At halftime, when the players ran off the court and the cheerleaders lined up to show off their newest routines, the five of us stayed put and talked about music. Actually, Lovejoy and I didn't say anything. Mandy stood and turned around to face Rob, and Kevin moved down to stand beside her so he could get in on their conversation. Must be nice to be so thick-headed you don't have a clue when somebody doesn't want you around.

Then, just like that, Lovejoy undid the straps on her leg brace and stood up.

"What're you doing?" I leaned forward. "Should you do that?"

She shoved the brace under the bleacher where she'd stashed her crutches. Then she turned to face me. "This is embarrassing. There's nothing wrong with my knee."

"What?"

Rob stood. "Hey, Mandy, let's go get—um, let's—"

"Yeah, great." They took off.

"It was a joke." Lovejoy actually had tears in her eyes. "A stupid joke. We thought it would be funny to pretend I got hurt today when you knocked me down. I did bruise my knee, but it's nothing."

I just stared at her.

"I was limping a little, so Rob's brother gave Mandy and me a ride home after school. I said something about how if it got worse, I could use the stuff from Mom's knee surgery. The brace and all. It just…just got out of control after that."

A tear slid down her cheek. She swiped at it with her fingers. "It seemed so hilarious when we were all in the car planning it out. It still seemed funny until I came in and saw your face. I could tell you were…"

She glanced at Kevin, who was gawking at her with his mouth hanging open. Then she looked at me again. "Bank, I'm sorry."

I didn't plan to get up and leave. I was halfway across the basketball court before I realized I had.

Cutting between two bouncing cheerleaders, I shoved through the crowd at the concession stand, straight out the door into the parking lot, and past the scattering of kids near the gym. I didn't look back.

Or maybe I did. I must have.

Because in my mind a jerky image played, like an old-time movie, of Lovejoy sitting down on the bleacher with both hands over her face.

8

Unlocking

I almost threw up.

If I'd let myself, I would have.

For years, I'd kept my emotions low-key. I had to, all the time. Because if it wasn't a habit, I couldn't keep it that way at home. I knew guys who talked trash with their friends and figured they could keep it clean around their parents or girlfriend—ha! Unless you keep something totally locked down, it's going to get out.

Lately, though, my lock hadn't worked so great. Maybe that was why Dad wanted me to get counseling.

A kind of psychiatric WD-40.

I stopped walking and laughed out loud. It wasn't all that funny, but if I didn't laugh, I might throw up after all. Or yell, or fall down, or rip the mirror off the car next to me. I might do all those things anyway. I wanted to destroy something, tear it to pieces, and that scared me but at the same time made me weirdly happy. Excited. For the first time, I understood why people went looking for trouble, to vandalize something or beat somebody up.

But I didn't *want* to understand that. And I sure didn't want to act on it.

I shoved both hands into my jeans pockets and started walking again.

If I hadn't driven myself to the game, I don't know what I would've done. Too far to walk home, especially in this cold wind with my jacket back in the gym. Maybe that would have motivated me to push through the worst of my tantrum and go back inside. Then I could've told Lovejoy everything was okay, and life would've returned to normal. I don't know. As it was, I headed for my car, intending to get in and drive.

Somewhere, anywhere. Not home. Not yet.

The gym lot had lights, but not enough. They didn't reach the far end where I'd parked. As I got to the Prizm, the asphalt under my feet gave way to the crunch of gravel. I stopped to scrape up a handful, reared back, and launched it into the night. Not a great throw. Along with the patter of rocks into grass came a few metallic clinks as they peppered my car. Probably the ones next to it, too.

From the narrow space by my passenger side came a weird noise. A sort of choking gargle.

I jerked around. On the dark ground by the front tire, a darker shadow made a quick, writhing movement. I heard it dragging itself along the gravel toward me. Something big.

My jumbled thoughts fused into one gigantic jolt of fear.

I slapped my hand down on the trunk of my car and vaulted over it to the driver's side. Not smart, maybe, since that put the thing between me and the gym. Straining my eyes into the night, squinting at one end of the car and then the other, back and forth, I fumbled in my jeans pocket for the keys.

Another possibility hit. What if the thing slithered under the car and got me by the legs?

I hopped from one foot to the other. "Come on, come on," I muttered. I could hear my keys jingling, but my fingers wouldn't close on them. The dancing didn't help.

With a sliding scatter of gravel, the thing burst out from between the cars and shot back toward the gym. I more heard than saw it go. I took off after it, thinking, *Danger, warn, protect!* All those kids hanging around just outside the gym, goofing off, smoking, making out. Unaware that something creepy was headed their way.

As it passed into the light, I saw streaming dark hair, a jacket,

38

legs. A person. Still running, the person glanced back.

Tara Prentiss?

"Hey!" I called. "What's wrong? Stop! Hey, Tara."

She kept going, and I kept chasing after her. But when I saw some of the people she'd been at the game with, I slowed down. Most had their backs to us, looking at something I couldn't see, but Alex and a couple of girls had turned to watch us. Tara ran up and joined them. Whatever had happened back by my car, she was safe now.

I stopped.

"Bank." Alex walked toward me. "What was that about?"

I shrugged. I was breathing hard, shaking from the adrenaline.

He frowned. "Were you *chasing* her?"

"No." My voice wobbled. I took a deep breath. "I mean, she was over by my car. She took off running. I thought something was wrong." I shrugged again. "I don't know what she was doing there."

He stared at me, still frowning. It did look bad, running after a girl in a dark parking lot. Great. The more I tried to explain, the worse it would look. Especially since I didn't *have* an explanation.

"Well, I guess she's okay. I'll just go back to my car." I gave a sort of awkward wave and turned away.

After I crossed into the dark edge of the parking lot, I looked back. Alex was still staring after me. I sucked in a deep breath and blew it out into the cold air, a cloud of fog disappearing into the night around my head.

I had a really bad feeling about this.

When I got to the Prizm, I stared at the place where she'd been. Then I took the flashlight out of my glove compartment and beamed it around. I even got down and looked under both cars.

Nothing. If somebody—or something—had attacked Tara here, they hadn't stayed around or left any obvious signs. What was going on with her?

I drove straight home after all.

My parents were in the living room. They looked up, obviously surprised to see me so early, but I just said, "I'm back," and took the stairs three at a time up to my room. They'd know something was wrong, but they'd also figure I would let them know if I wanted to talk. They were good about that. Even Dad.

As soon as I shut the door, I wished I hadn't come home.

My room was too small. Our house was too small. Our *town* was too small. I needed miles and miles of open space, where I could run and yell and send everything flying away. Life was crowding in on me, piling on top of me, and I couldn't do anything about it.

I paced around my room, wishing I had something to eat. My snack drawer was empty, and I didn't want to go downstairs. I didn't want to risk getting ambushed by a parent. I didn't want to see or talk to anybody.

Except Jeff. I wanted to talk to Jeff.

Thumping onto my chair, I heaved a sigh that blew a couple of papers across my desk. Email just wouldn't do it tonight. With life dumping on me like this, I needed to talk to Jeff, let him peel a few layers off so I could breathe again.

One problem, though. Jeff had lost his cell phone just before he moved. His parents were making him pay for the next one, since this made the third time he'd done that. Even great guys have their weak points. His family didn't have a land line, since everybody used their cell phones, which left Jeff incommunicado—there's a great word—until he could save up enough money. All we had until then was email.

I checked my inbox. Junk, junk, and more junk. Nothing from Jeff yet, which might mean he'd gone out with the flower girl tonight. I sat staring at the screen for a long time, then typed:

To: jeffers@moondog.com
From: bankrobber@cvc.org
Subject:

Hey Jefferson. Great game tonight, Tim Buckland just couldn't miss. Maybe North will actually go to State this year.

Later $

No, tonight email just wouldn't do it.

I pulled on my pajamas, turned off my phone, and crawled into bed. I stared up at the ceiling. I'd been so sure this would be the greatest week of my life, what with turning sixteen and getting my license.

Yeah, right.

The best thing about this week would be leaving it behind.

9

Changes

Monday morning I woke up feeling so much better, I couldn't believe I was the same person.

In the shower, I thought about Lovejoy hobbling into the gym with crutches and that ridiculous, bulky leg brace. Left over from her mom's surgery, she'd said. I could understand hanging onto a pair of crutches, but a leg brace? What else did Lovejoy's parents have stuffed into their closets? I actually starting laughing and swallowed a mouthful of soapy water.

She and Mandy and Rob had fooled me, all right. What an idiot. Too bad my idiocy ruined the joke for everybody. I'd have to apologize, at least to Lovejoy.

"Bank, you look so happy," Mom said when I came down for breakfast.

Her voice sounded little and young. I looked again. One hand curled around a glass of milk, and the other cupped her elbow.

"Oh, hi, Libby. Yeah, I feel great."

"You *reckonized* me." She smiled shyly, looking pleased. Libby was a four-year-old alter who came out only when things felt especially safe. I hadn't seen her in a while, which probably had more to do with me than her.

Her smile faded, and she gazed at me with round, earnest eyes. "I thought you were sick. You didn't go to church yesterday."

"No. Not really. I just needed to get caught up on my sleep. How was church?"

"*I* don't know." Her expression went reproachful, her bottom lip poking out. She tucked both hands under her arms. "You know I don't come out with all those people. Meredith was there."

"Sorry. I just thought she might've told you."

"She sat by that lady. The one that comes here sometimes. I stayed inside, but I could still hear her. She laughs *so loud.*"

Mrs. Jennings. I grinned. "She's a nice lady."

She nodded. "Fighter came out once. She thought somebody was being mean to Meredith. But that lady was nice to her, so she went back in."

That must've been interesting for Mrs. Jennings. And for everyone else around them.

I'd spent the whole weekend in bed with my phone off and my blinds shut, getting up only when the kitchen or bathroom called my name. I'd seen Mom maybe a couple of times, Dad not at all. I hadn't gotten on the computer or looked at homework. I'd done nothing except sleep.

And now I felt great. Maybe my whole problem lately had just been sleep deprivation. In P.E. last week, Coach Summers had handed out a list of *Ten Terrible Habits of Teens*, and number one on the list read: *Not enough sleep.* Number two: *Too much fast food.*

Guilty on both counts. No joke. Maybe I should find that list and see what else I ought to change.

Over the weekend, the temperature had dropped even more and the wind had picked up. I pulled my jacket out of the coat closet. Not until I'd zipped it up and headed out the door did I remember I'd left this jacket in the gym Friday night. Somebody must have dropped it off.

Probably Rob and Kevin. Could've been Lovejoy, but that didn't seem likely.

Whatever, I was happy to have it. The Prizm's heater had decided to sleep in this morning, a choice it made two or three times a week. The air wheezing through the vents had barely hit lukewarm by the time I got to school. Then the walk from the parking lot froze me again. It felt great to leave the drafty first floor hallway and climb the stairs into the stuffy, smelly warmth of the second floor.

I jammed my jacket into the six square inches allowed for it, not even glancing toward Tara's locker. No way would I get caught staring again.

The more I thought about Friday night, the more I wanted to know what happened to her in the parking lot. Maybe Rob knew by now. He seemed to pick news like that out of the air. But if he didn't say anything, I wouldn't ask.

Better to just stay out of it.

As I headed for first-hour Spanish, my thoughts swung to Lovejoy. I looked forward to seeing her. Apologizing wasn't my favorite activity, but it would be worth it. I wanted to watch her brown eyes sparkle and her lips curve into that curly smile, once she knew I'd gotten over being mad and actually thought their prank was funny. I could tell her we were even now. I'd knocked her down, and she'd ruined a great basketball game for me.

Of course, she hadn't exactly enjoyed the game either.

I figured I'd have to wait until sixth hour when we both had biology. But as I turned the corner, here she came with Mandy.

"Oh, *cripes*," I said.

This was too much. All my good humor and regret about hurting Lovejoy's feelings the other night drained away. This girl just didn't know when to stop.

She had the crutches again.

"Bank," she called. "Hey, Bank!"

I looked away and kept walking, angling off to the right so other kids made a moving barricade between us. The last thing I expected was for Mandy to come charging across the hall, grabbing my arm and shaking it like a furious little dog with a chew toy. She didn't use her teeth, of course. But for a second, I thought she might.

"What's your problem?" I demanded.

"What's *yours*?" She glared up at me. "It's your fault Lovejoy's on crutches, and you don't even have the decency—"

"*My* fault? Hey, we've already been through this. She told

44

me her leg was okay, remember?"

"That was a joke. This isn't."

"No kidding. There's nothing funny…" I stopped. "What do you mean, this isn't a joke?"

"Well, it isn't. She was so upset when you ran off at halftime, she went out after you and tripped over one of those parking things."

"Parking things?"

"You know, that concrete thing that stops you when you park the car. She fell over one of those."

Oh. Come to think of it, I didn't know what that was called either. Though you weren't actually supposed to use it to *stop* the car. I had a feeling Mandy would be a scary driver. "She broke her leg?"

Mandy let go of my arm. "Sprained her ankle."

"Oh," I said, relieved.

"It's a *bad* sprain. Sprains hurt worse than breaks, and they can take a long time to heal. She's in a *lot* of pain. And walking with crutches isn't fun, you know."

"She should've thought of that the first time."

I didn't know why I said it. I wasn't mad at Lovejoy anymore. And I did feel bad about what happened to her, though I didn't think it was my fault. I hadn't asked her to come chasing after me and fall over a parking thing.

Mandy had been gazing earnestly up at me. Now her face went hard, and she pulled back. "Wow. Lovejoy was sure wrong about *you*."

She turned her back on me and marched across the hall to where Lovejoy waited, propped on her crutches. They started forward, Mandy talking a mile a minute.

I made a move to follow, then stopped. What was the point? Every time Lovejoy Fox and I ran into each other, life got worse. For both of us.

Third-hour math was right next door to my second-hour computer lab. Early in the school year, I'd gotten in the habit of waiting in the hall for Rob and Kevin so we could walk into math together. I don't know why. It was just something I did.

Today, leaning against the wall by the doorway, watching people go past, I wondered if Lovejoy would come this way again.

I hoped not. I didn't remember seeing her here before last Friday. Kids almost always went the same way every day, the shortest distance between one class and the next. Maybe she'd had something unusual going that day. Or maybe she'd changed her usual route so she and Mandy could walk together. Maybe she *would* come around the corner any second.

I kicked my book bag closer to the wall. So what? If she came by, she came by. If she made eye contact, I'd smile. If she didn't, I wouldn't.

Kids went past me into the classroom. The early few, the middle many. I glanced at the hall clock. It looked like Rob and Kevin were going to be part of the last-minute trickle. What was taking them so long? The Bee buzzed past, a pad of pink tardy slips clutched in one hand. I leaned around to peer into the room and see if the guys had somehow made it here ahead of me. Nope.

When I swung back, they were just coming around the corner. Rob walked beside Mandy. Behind them, Lovejoy struggled along on her crutches, talking to Kevin.

The two girls went past me like I was a smudge on the wall.

The guys peeled off from them, saying, "Bye, see you later." As he went into the room, Rob met my eyes but didn't smile. Kevin slid me a look I read as sorry-but-what-can-I-do and slouched in behind him.

Of course.

The wall pressed against my back, smooth and hard. Rob and Mandy. Their hokey lion tamer act on the bleachers. The two of them running off together at halftime. How could I have forgotten how goofy they'd acted at the game? If I'd remembered, maybe I would've been ready for this.

Everybody was taking sides. Against me.

I half turned, pushing away from the wall, ready to head down the stairs and out the front door.

Miles and miles of open space, where I could run and yell and let everything go flying away.

I stopped.

If I'd learned one thing from all these years with my mom, it was this. Running away doesn't work. It just doesn't. Running away means you have to come back and face it later, which by then is ten times harder. If you hang in there long enough, though, things will change.

One way or another.

Above my head, the intercom burped and crackled, which meant the drop-dead bell was about to sound. I picked up my book bag and went in. I passed Rob and Kevin without looking at them and squeezed into a desk at the back of the room.

Mrs. Adams was already handing out last week's test. Then she went over the whole thing, talking to us like we were third graders, the way she always did after a really bad one. I didn't listen. I was thinking about running away.

Not as in planning to do it. More as in realizing that was exactly what had happened Friday night at the game.

First Rob and Mandy had deserted, like rats off a sinking ship, when they saw Lovejoy was going to tell me the truth. Then I did the same thing to her, running off to my car. The only ones who hadn't acted like cowards were Lovejoy because she was brave, and Kevin because he was clueless.

It probably wouldn't have changed anything if Rob and

Mandy had stayed. But if I had, everything would be different. I'd been a coward and a quitter. And not just then. If I hadn't run away from Lovejoy this morning—

"Bank." Mrs. Adams sounded grim.

Uh-oh. What now? What had I missed?

But when I looked up, she actually smiled at me. That happened maybe once a semester. I wasn't expecting it this early in the year.

"Since you seem to be the only student who understands this concept—" she shot a death-ray glare at the rest of the class, "—would you please come to the whiteboard and write it out?"

This could be bad, since I had no idea what she was talking about. But when I got to the board, clutching my test, she said, "Number seven. Show your work."

She had me explain it, too. Embarrassing, but at least it was just numbers. I like words, but they can get you in a lot more trouble.

When Mrs. Adams nodded for me to go back to my seat, I couldn't help glancing at Rob and Kevin. Rob just stared at the board, pretending I wasn't right there in front of it. Kevin grinned and gave me a thumbs up where Rob couldn't see. While I tried to decide if I should smile back or not, my mouth went ahead and did it for me.

Probably a good choice.

I sat down feeling a little better. I just had to keep remembering. If you hang in there long enough, things will change.

One way or another.

10

Connections

The three of us always walked to the cafeteria and ate lunch together. But this time, Rob and Kevin were already halfway down the stairs by the time I got out the door. In the cafeteria, I bought three cheeseburgers and a drink. I automatically looked around to see where they were sitting, before it hit me I was now on my own. In the worst place in the world to be when you have *no friends*.

There I stood, the giant cooked noodle, looming taller and taller as I hovered in the middle of the cafeteria with a tray in my hands and nowhere to sit.

I might have given the guys a try, even at the risk of public rejection. But Rob was sitting next to Mandy, with Kevin squeezed in beside him. I didn't see Lovejoy, but everyone else at the table made up part of Alex White's group. I definitely didn't belong there. Not after Friday night.

Which left me with three choices.

One. Run away. I already knew that wouldn't work.

Two. Sit at the loser table and make it official I was one of them.

Three. Sneak out and hide in the computer lab. Mr. Lattup wasn't a nerd, but you could tell he used to be one. This probably explained why he liked me. If he came in and caught me eating lunch in the lab, I wouldn't get in trouble.

Stuffing the cheeseburgers into the top of my book bag, I wedged the drink in more carefully, dropped my tray on the moving belt, and headed for the cafeteria exit. As I got close, I slowed. Three guys were blocking the doorway so a scared-looking girl with zits and posture issues couldn't get out.

"Move." I used my deepest voice, hoping I sounded more confident than I felt.

They moved. Being tall had its advantages, though a few more muscles would've helped. On my own, I might have stood there without saying anything until they got bored and went away, but I hate seeing kids pick on somebody like that. Talk about mean girls. Guys can be just as bad.

The girl stayed close to me until we got safely past. She slid a quick look up at me. Then her head went down and she scurried away.

The lab was empty. Mr. Laptop, as everybody called him—he said he didn't mind, and by now some kids actually thought it was his name—had left the ancient radio he was always tinkering with tuned to the jazz station. He'd set the volume just high enough to hear. Peaceful, after the ear-breaking crowd scene down in the cafeteria. I could get used to this.

While I ate, I checked email for the first time since Friday night. Junk, forwards, group emails. One from Jeff, with nothing in the subject line. I deleted everything else and opened his.

"Whoa."

I set my cheeseburger down and leaned forward to stare at the screen. In his whole life, Jeff had never written this much at one time. I didn't know he could.

To: bankrobber@cvc.org
From: jeffers@moondog.com
Subject:

Rose Brownlee. Talk about the perfect name. She has long brown hair and blue eyes with these sort of brown speckles, and she has this natural rose color on her cheeks and lips and the sweetest smile you ever saw. She's quiet but not because she's shy, it's more like she watches and listens and only talks when she has something to say instead of blahblahblah.

No, I'm not going to knock her down. It might work for you but it's not my style. Yesterday after class I told Rose how much I liked her singing and that I play the trumpet. I asked if she wanted to get a pizza or something. She said her brother was in a play and she was going with her family, but they had an extra ticket if I wanted to go too. I opened my mouth to say no but yes came out.

How's that for a scary first date? The whole family!

I figured it must be a school play, Hansel and Gretel or something, but turns out it's her older brother who's with a professional touring company. We saw some Russian tragedy I can't even pronounce. Her brother was great though, and I liked her parents and sisters.

Rose is into genealogy and she's going to do my family tree. She says every part of you is important and your past is a big part of your present. Maybe you should find out who's hanging on your branches.

Rose is so sweet, you've got to meet her. Not going to say it yet, but I think I'm in _ _ _ _☺☺☺☺

J.

Jeff, doing smiley faces? Using the word *sweet*? Twice, even. Writing about this girl as if somebody had opened a word hydrant and couldn't shut it off?

I checked the date. Saturday, which meant they must've gone to the play Friday night. For such a slow guy, Jeff had moved incredibly fast after seeing her in the talent show on Wednesday.

Well, good for him. At least one of us had some relational skills.

I ate my cheeseburger while I read his letter through again. Then I typed:

To: jeffers@moondog.com
From: bankrobber@cvc.org
Subject:

Hey Jefferson. Rose sounds great. Happy for you bro.

I won't go into a lot of boring detail but I did something stupid, big surprise, and hurt Lovejoy's feelings. Because of Lovejoy her friend Mandy's mad at me. Because of Mandy Rob's mad at me. Because of Rob Kevin's not mad, just not around. He'd rather be with them and I don't blame him. Right now I don't even like being with me.

Guess you should be glad you moved to the frozen north.

Hey, new word. Peccadillo. It means things other people don't like about each other. I must have tons of peccadilloes. Not sure I want to know what's hanging on my family tree.

Your peccadillo is phones. You'd better save your $
for a new one instead of spending it all on dates
with Rose.

Later $

I almost deleted everything after *bro* but then went ahead and
sent it. Right away, I wished I hadn't. For one thing, I sounded
pathetic. For another, Jeff was the only person who didn't know
what a loser I was.

And here I had to go and tell him myself.

By Wednesday, I'd started packing a lunch so I could go straight to
the computer lab. Good old faithful peanut butter sandwiches. You
don't need a refrigerator or microwave, and they stick with you all
afternoon.

When "Rudolph the Red-Nosed Reindeer" started up in my
jeans pocket, I fumbled my first sandwich and almost dropped it on
the keyboard where I was writing to Jeff. *That* could've been bad. I
scooted my chair back and pulled out my phone. Still chewing, I
flipped it open.

"Bank? It's Dad."

I knew that, thanks to caller ID. But Dad's screen had gone
blank a few weeks earlier, time-travelling him back to the days when
you picked up at your own risk. Since he couldn't see, it was like he
assumed nobody else could. I usually played along.

"Oh. Hey, Dad. What's up?"

"Your voice sounds odd."

"Lunch." I swallowed. "I'm eating."

"I expected to get your voicemail. You shouldn't have your phone on at school."

"Yeah, I forgot to turn it off. But nobody ever calls me during school hours." Or any other time.

His grunt sounded doubtful. "Well, I won't keep you. I meant to remind you last night. Don't forget your appointment today."

Wednesday. Viking Clone. I groaned.

"Make sure you go. Don't waste his time."

"I'll go. And I *won't* waste his time."

"I meant—" He stopped. "Good enough. I'll see you tonight, Bank."

"Bye," I mumbled.

The connection went dead. Some kids' dads say things like, "I love you, son," when they hang up. Not mine.

In my email to Jeff, I grouched about having to go see Viking Clone. But the idea of being around somebody who would actually talk to me had started to sound good. Even if he *was* being paid to do it.

Jeff had gone from writing his all-time longest email to hyper-short ones I found annoying.

To: bankrobber@cvc.org
From: jeffers@moondog.com
Subject:

That had shown up on Monday, two days ago. I'd given it way more attention than it deserved. Did it mean my last email sounded as pitiful as I thought, and Jeff was poking me for being such a crybaby? Or was the frowny face supposed to show sincere sympathy?

Of course, it might just mean that when he told me about Rose and put in all the smiley faces, he discovered the frowny ones, too. I didn't even know my computer would do those. I'd never thought about trying.

And why didn't he just put the frowny face in the subject line? That way I wouldn't bother opening it.

I'd finally decided not to answer, since I wasn't sure what to say.

Tuesday's had been just as bad.

To: bankrobber@cvc.org
From: jeffers@moondog.com
Subject:

☹ ☺ ?

I didn't answer that one, either.

Today I'd decided to go ahead and write him, but I didn't mention the faces. I just told him about the Prizm's wonky heater, and Trish Vespers wanting me to tell him hi for her again, and how the people who bought his old house had told Dad they were going to paint it sage, whatever that was. Boring stuff like that. And, of course, about Dad's phone call just now.

Jeff's latest email popped up in my inbox right after I sent mine to him. Either cyberspace delay, or Jeff was on a school computer, too.

I opened it and groaned.

To: bankrobber@cvc.org
From: jeffers@moondog.com
Subject:

☹ !

"Oh, come on, Jeff," I said. This was getting ridiculous.

I leaned back in my chair, picked up my second sandwich,

and stared at the grumpy little circle on the computer screen.

True, right now frowny faces fit my situation a lot better than smiley ones. For the first time in my life, I had no local friends at all.

None. Zero. Zilch. Nada.

I'd never been the kind of person to run around with a big group, but I usually had two or three guys I could call friends. Sometimes Jeff had been the only one, but I could live with that. I had him to talk to at school and hang out with afterwards, and that was all I needed. But now Jeff was in the frozen north with Rose, falling in _ _ _ _ ☺☺☺☺

I wondered when he was actually going to say the word.

I wondered when he was going to say *any* words.

11

Shrinking

"I know a girl at school who's got DID."

Viking Clone's neutral-but-receptive expression didn't even twitch. Disappointing. I'd hoped for a reaction.

I took a big swallow of my Dr Pepper and set the bottle on the carpet. Maybe I should take it as a challenge to shake him out of neutral, give it a solid try every session. By the time we finished for good—whatever that was supposed to look like—I would get at least one honestly astonished expression out of him.

Glancing at the picture over his desk, I decided the cows didn't look so much worried today as interested. They liked the idea, too.

He reached for the recorder. "Is that what you want to talk about today?"

The brave set of Lovejoy's shoulders above the colorful ribbons on her crutches. Jeff, far, far away in the frozen north. Rob and Kevin. Eating lunch by myself in the computer lab. My life as a pathetic loser.

I shrugged. "Sure."

He waited, hand poised over the recorder.

It took me a second to catch on. I pumped enthusiasm into my voice. "Yeah, definitely. That's what I want to talk about."

Another long moment slid by.

"All right." His finger popped the button down with a decisive snap. As he leaned back, his chair creaked louder than ever.

I definitely should've brought the WD-40.

57

Viking Clone didn't seem to notice. Or if he did, it didn't bother him. Even his hands looked NBR, one resting on top of the other, fingers spread loosely just above his knee.

I stared down at my hands, balled into fists on the arms of my chair. I'd picked a different chair today, squashy and fat and incredibly ugly, covered with gigantic pink and purple flowers found nowhere in nature. My big fists with their bony knuckles looked ridiculous against the fussy fabric.

To get a person's real reaction, watch his hands.

I'd just read about that in the waiting room. The article in *Modern Psychology* said even people with perfect control over their facial expressions gave themselves away with how their hands reacted. Startled, scared, mad, tense, excited. If you knew what you were looking for, you could see it. Maybe I should say something like, "This morning I killed my dad and hid his body in the garage," just to see what Viking Clone's hands would do.

Bad idea. He'd decide I really had problems.

I flexed my fingers and studied them.

Mom's hands told me a lot. Sometimes I could even tell which alter was out that way. Libby's fingers looked weak and childish, curled in. Fighter was big on fists. Truth touched things, running her fingertips over them like she was feeling the texture. Hope never fumbled or dropped anything. And Mom's left hand always moved a certain way when someone else wanted to come out. That was Gatekeeper, deciding whether or not to let them.

Until Gatekeeper, I had to run after my mom a lot. We'd be at a store or the park or somewhere, and someone else would come out, get scared, and take off. So I'd take off after them. Since everyone except Meredith was little, nobody could run very fast, so it wasn't hard to catch them. But it *was* embarrassing. Especially as I got older.

Finally, her therapist suggested everybody inside should elect someone to decide who could come out, and when. That was when I first met Gatekeeper. He did a pretty good job. He decided if it was safe, depending on where Mom was and who else was around.

I was always safe.

As for Dad—

"Are you sure this is what you want to talk about, Bank?"

Startled, I looked up and caught the clock's reflection in the cow picture. "Wow, sorry. I didn't mean to take so long. I was, well, I guess I was thinking."

"Think all you want," he said. "It's your time."

Okay. If I knew about the hand principle, Viking Clone sure did. He had probably read the same article. And fists were *not* good. I picked up my Dr Pepper, took a long drink, and set it back on the floor. I flopped that hand over the arm of my chair and rested the other on my leg, even more relaxed than his.

"Yeah, well. That girl at school," I said. "The one with DID." I kept an eye on his hands. Maybe I wasn't the only North High student spending time in Viking Clone's inner sanctum. "Her name's Tara Prentiss."

No reaction. A full minute ticked by before he asked, "What makes you think she has DID?"

So I told him what I'd seen, which wasn't much. Just four short episodes. That first time outside the school office. The next day at her locker. Friday night when she first got to the basketball game. And the big one, halftime in the parking lot.

"I didn't recognize it at first," I said. "But it's exactly like with my mom. Not just her eyes, or the look on her face, but the way she carries herself and moves and everything. For just a second, she's somebody else. Scared and little—you know, young—but checking to see if I'm safe. Just like Gatekeeper for my mom."

He nodded. I'd already told him about Gatekeeper.

"Then, *pop!* and the supermodel's back." I grinned, feeling awkward. I hadn't meant to let that one out. "She's really gorgeous, and she acts so confident. That's why I call her the supermodel."

He nodded again.

I reached for my Dr Pepper. "If I wasn't so used to my mom,

I probably wouldn't have noticed anything those first three times. But that night in the parking lot..." Just thinking about the strangled sounds coming out of the darkness gave me the willies. "That was weird. Creepy."

"What do you think happened that night?"

"I figure some guy put the moves on her and got too pushy. Or somebody said something that triggered her, and she went and hid. And then that gravel I threw would scare her even more. So she ran." I shrugged. "I don't know. It seems funny, like too much of a coincidence. That my mom would have DID, I mean, and then I'd meet somebody else who does. It's not exactly common."

"True." He shifted in his chair. "But take a young child, subject her to severe and ongoing abuse, and dissociation *is* likely to happen. I think we're going to find it's more common than we'd realized."

An opinion! That was a first.

"So." I sat straighter. "Do you think it sounds like DID?"

"It's possible." He crossed his legs and cupped one hand over his knee. The fingers tapped twice, then stopped. "I'm not saying that's what it is, of course. You have a car, right?"

"A car? Well, yeah. A white Prizm." Was this some kind of trick question? The Prizm wasn't really *my* car, as in paying for it or having the title in my name. Or even choosing it. If the choice was up to me, I'd pick out something bigger I didn't have to cram myself into.

"Suppose your car has a problem with overheating." His chair creaked as he leaned forward. "Whenever the engine gets hot, it gives off a certain smell. At that point, you know you need to stop and let it cool down." He gave me an are-you-with-me look that could have come straight off Dad's face.

"Okay," I said.

"Now, suppose you're riding in a friend's car. You become aware of that same smell. What do you think?"

Not the happiest question he could've asked, considering my

friend count was currently at zero. I flipped the mental calendar back a week to when Rob and Kevin had still been around. Neither one could drive yet, but this was all rhetorical anyway. "I guess I'd figure my friend's car had the same problem."

"And what's your friend thinking?"

That depended. If it was Kevin...

"Probably nothing," I said.

That almost got a smile. Not quite, but close. "Maybe. Or your friend might notice the smell, but he doesn't know what it means. You do. You're the expert on this, because you've lived with it."

"Okay."

"In the same way," he said, "you have a lifetime of experience with your mother. If someone in your school does dissociate, other students might notice an occasional odd behavior. But you'll recognize it for what it is."

That made sense. I could have gotten it without all the car analogy, though.

I drank the last of my Dr Pepper and screwed the lid back on. "It's sad, you know. This girl is so gorgeous, every guy at school is interested. But if she does have DID, she'll never have a real life."

"Why do you say that?"

"Well, look at my mom. Dad has to be so careful all the time. I mean, she takes care of the house, and usually she's okay to drive and run errands and everything, but..." I shrugged.

We sat in silence. The clock ticked. The cows stared gloomily at the tree.

Finally he said, "Bank, have you read much about DID? Recent medical articles, written by experts with plenty of hands-on experience?"

I shook my head. "I read some a few years ago. I don't know why I quit. Too depressing, I guess."

"What do you know about the statistics for recovery?"

I balanced the empty bottle on my knee. "They're not good."

61

He leaned forward. "They *are* good. Seventy percent or higher."

"To do what? Not kill yourself?"

I wanted to shove the words back inside my mouth. I stared down at my hands. Fists again, balled up tighter than ever. This time, I didn't bother changing them. My knuckles looked red, scraped, as if I'd been punching something. Or someone.

"Much more than that," he said. "Complete healing, with total integration of the alters, so you have one person living a normal, happy life. As normal and happy as the rest of us, that is."

When I looked up, his eyes were serious. Intent.

He shook his head. "It's not a perfect world, Bank. We all have scars. People with DID can learn how to carry those scars and have lives worth living, just like anyone else."

It sounded great. But I didn't believe it.

The empty bottle tipped sideways. I caught it and tossed it under my chair. "Dr. Kind, Mom's been in counseling since before I was born. And she still isn't normal. Things are better now, sure. But even if she got total recovery tomorrow, she'd be like almost forty. Her life is basically over. Is that what it'll be like for Tara?"

A smiled flicked across his face, though I wasn't sure why.

"I can't tell you that, of course," he said. "What I *can* tell you is that the specialist working with your mother now is excellent. Gifted. You have no idea how fortunate your family is that Dr. Samuelson moved here—"

The last word jerked, as if he'd stopped himself from saying more. I might not have noticed, except that both of his thumbs jerked, too.

For a second, I was puzzled. Then I got it. *Aha.* He didn't think much of Mom's other shrink, the one she'd gone to all those years. In giving her new shrink the thumbs up, he'd just given the old one the thumbs down. Literally.

When I glanced at the picture, I could've sworn the smaller cow winked at me. We would never get Viking Clone to admit it, but the cows and I knew.

I'd just outshrunk my shrink.

12

Giraffe

My mind was on food.

Cheeseburgers. French fries smothered in melted cheese and chili. Crunchy, greasy onion rings. Health food.

As I left Viking Clone's restroom, I pulled out my wallet. Then, without bothering to open it, I crammed it back into my pocket. I already knew what was in there. I had exactly seven cents, which explained why I hadn't stopped at Sonic today on the way here. I wouldn't be stopping on the way home, either.

"Thanks a lot, Dad," I said aloud.

Instead of taking the hallway to the reception area, today I opted to go out the side of the building. The bar on the self-locking metal door clanked as I shoved it harder than I needed to. Cold air swirled in.

Just outside the door, I spotted a penny on the sidewalk. I picked it up. "Well, yay. That gets me up to eight cents." Tossing the coin from hand to hand, I headed for the front parking lot. My stomach grumbled with every step.

Thanks a whole lot, Dad.

Signing me up for a student "Save-Don't-Spend" account had accomplished my dad's goal of getting me to keep my money locked up in savings, whether I wanted to or not. This had to be the most limited bank account in the world. No ATM, no debit card, no checks, and only two withdrawals per month—which had to be done at the main branch on the other side of town. No wonder I kept running out of cash.

I flipped the penny high into the air and caught it.

Okay, so this wasn't all my dad's fault. Spending down to my last few cents was one of my peccadilloes, the same way I didn't fill up the Prizm until it was running on fumes. Dad had gotten onto me about both of those. Someday, he said, I would regret my "short-sighted foolishness."

I regretted it now. I was starving.

Rounding the corner to the front sidewalk with my mind on my stomach, I vaguely registered someone coming toward me from the far side of the building. Then, one after another, in a sort of mental stutter, the details came clear.

Girl.

Shiny dark hair.

Sea-green sweater.

Perfect figure.

Tara Prentiss.

No way.

Absolutely no way.

Tara hadn't seen me yet. She was looking down, digging in her purse the way girls do. My legs didn't even bother to check with my brain. They just skidded to a stop, backpedaled, and bounced me out of sight around the corner, where I flattened myself against the wall.

No way.

Tara Prentiss. And here I'd just told Viking Clone I didn't believe in coincidences.

I waited until I couldn't stand the suspense. As I peered around the corner, a maroon Volvo pulled up beside Tara, facing me. She stepped off the curb, her dark hair floating in the breeze, and reached for the front passenger door.

I ducked back again.

What next?

I looked around. From the front parking lot, a driveway ran along my side of the building, out through overflow parking and

65

onto Baker Street. If the Volvo turned left and went out the way it came in, I'd be okay. But if it turned right, Tara couldn't miss seeing the six-foot-four-inch cooked noodle from North High, lurking by the corner, obviously hiding. The guy who'd already chased her through the gym parking lot at night.

Not only that, but the woman driving the Volvo looked like a mother. Tara's mother. I could just hear Tara's voice if they did come this way. "Mom! That's the creepy guy who..."

It might not happen. The Volvo might turn left instead of right.

But this was no time to wait around and see.

As I heard the solid thump of a car door closing, I pushed away from the wall and headed back the way I'd come. No more cooked noodle. Now I felt more like a giraffe chased by lions.

Head up, arms and legs pumping, I galloped past one ugly metal door after another. I passed Viking Clone's office and kept going, all the way to the far end of the building. Cutting right, I flailed along the back and threw myself around the corner to the other side.

Nothing here but a narrow sidewalk, stubby bushes, and a wooden privacy fence. Which meant no chance of the maroon Volvo showing up.

Safe.

Breathing fast, I leaned against the brick wall of the building. Either I'd overdosed on adrenaline, like the other night in the parking lot, or I was way out of shape. Not enough physical exercise. One of the *Ten Terrible Habits of*—

The metal door beside me popped open. A woman with short gray hair stepped out, a jacket dangling from one hand.

"Oh." She barely caught the door before it could close and lock her out. "I was looking for—have you seen—" She shook her head. "Never mind. I'm sorry if I startled you."

I took a deep breath. "No problem."

She glanced down the sidewalk both ways, then turned back

66

to me. "Do you need help?"

I must've looked ridiculous, plastered against the wall, panting like an overheated giraffe. "No thanks. I was just running. Guess I'm a little out of shape."

True, at least mostly. But lame. Nobody goes running in jeans.

"Are you sure?"

"Yeah," I said. "I really am okay."

The way her eyes scanned me, as if she could see into the back of my calorie-starved brain, reminded me of Viking Clone. She made a *hmmm* sound and said, "Yes, I can see that. Well, enjoy your marathon." She looked down the sidewalk again before she ducked back inside. The door clunked shut behind her.

I sucked in another breath and peeled myself off the wall. The whole encounter had taken maybe a minute. But that was enough for me to recognize the leather jacket the woman held.

Tara's. It had to be Tara's jacket. She must have been in that office and came out that door about the time I went out the opposite side of the building. We'd both walked toward the front and turned the corner toward each other at the same time.

Thinking hard, I headed for the front of the building.

How could I find out whose office this was? None of these exterior doors had labels. The ones along the inside hallway did, but since Viking Clone hung out in the other half of the building, I had no way to look. The receptionist would never buzz me down that hallway.

None of my business, but I wanted to know. What if I just went back in to the receptionist's desk, pointed at the door to the right, and said, "Excuse me, but could you tell me who has the last office on that side?"

She'd think I was crazy.

I grinned. After all, this *was* a building full of shrinks. She must've heard questions a lot crazier than that. I trotted up the steps to the front door and pulled on the handle. It didn't budge.

"Did you forget something?"

The voice sounded small and crackly and seemed to be talking to my elbow. It was like being in an animated movie where a mouse or bug makes friends with the human character.

"Hello, Bank," the voice said. "Look up."

I tipped my head back. A security camera above the door waggled at me.

"Did you forget something? I lock the door after five." The receptionist, her voice distorted by the intercom beside the door. I'd never even noticed it before.

I hadn't planned what to say. It just came out. "My friend left her jacket. A brown leather—"

"In Dr. Sam's office? Sure, I have it here at the desk. Dr. Sam brought it up just a second ago. Come on in."

The door buzzed. I pulled it open and stepped into the entryway, then pushed through that door to the reception area. I'd never paid much attention to the woman at the desk before, but this time I read her nameplate. Tiffany. She looked too old for the name, but I guess even Tiffanys have to hit middle age sometime.

"Thanks." I took the jacket she held out. "How'd you know who I was? That was kind of weird."

She laughed. "You're distinctive, Bank. I don't remember everybody, but you stand out."

Big surprise. Six-foot-four-inch cooked noodles tend to do that.

I pointed over my shoulder. "So, can I get back out?"

"Of course. Fire regulations. You just can't get in once you're out. Not unless I let you in."

Outside of school, I'd never seen a building with so many rules. No smoking, no running, no weapons, and so on. And when you were in Viking Clone's waiting room, a sign on the door of his sanctum read: IF THE THERAPIST IS MORE THAN 5 MINUTES LATE FOR YOUR APPOINTMENT, PLEASE GO OUT AND TELL THE RECEPTIONIST. DO <u>NOT</u> KNOCK ON THIS DOOR.

In other words, if he ran late coming out to get you, it was probably because the client before you had freaked out. He didn't want you banging on the door and making things worse.

I loved that sign. I wanted one for my room.

"Well, thanks, um, Tiffany. See you next week." I waved awkwardly and headed out.

The temperature was dropping along with the sun. I jogged to my car, started the engine, and tried the heater. This time, it warmed up right away. Then I sat and stared down at Tara's jacket. It looked so little, folded on my front passenger seat. She wasn't all that short, not compared to other girls, but she was slender. Fragile.

Something stirred in my chest. I took a deep breath.

Maybe Tara didn't have DID.

She might just be shy. Maybe what I'd taken for dissociation just meant her self-assured facade had slipped for a second, letting the insecurity show. Lots of kids tried to look more confident than they felt. Probably everyone. I sure did.

That night in the parking lot, though…

What if some guy really had jumped her? Hurt her. She could've even passed out. That would explain the weird sounds as she came to, and why she ran. She'd be confused, disoriented, scared. That could also explain why she was seeing a shrink now, to work through the trauma.

I reached over to touch her jacket. Something slid out of my sleeve and dropped onto the leather.

"Huh." I picked it up. "How'd *you* get there?"

In all my running and jumping around, the penny I'd found outside Viking Clone's office must have somehow gone up my sleeve. As I held it up to look at the date, the copper glinted in the low rays of the setting sun. Last year, 2004.

Which, considering the way things had been going lately, promised to be the last halfway decent year of my life.

On impulse, I slid the penny into a pocket of Tara's jacket.

As I drove home, questions and ideas fired themselves at me

from every direction, like missiles in a computer war game where I was the whole world's target. I dodged them all.

I'd have to deal with them sometime, sure. But first I needed food.

13

Exoduster

Big excitement when I got home.

Five of Mom's alters had integrated. First time ever, and she was still humming with reaction.

"I thought it would be sad having somebody go in for good," she told me while I microwaved leftover lasagna. "Like losing a friend, or a child. But it isn't like that at all. They're still here, but now they're with me all the time, really *part* of me. I feel so happy."

"But you're crying," I pointed out.

She smiled, brown eyes sparkling behind the tears. "You don't understand women, do you, Bank?"

That was for sure. "No."

The microwave beeped. Dad had taken an out-of-town client to dinner, so Mom and I were on our own tonight. With all the excitement, she didn't feel much like cooking, which made this a good time to clear out some leftovers. I'd snagged the lasagna and loaded up.

"So, what was it like?" I carried my plate to the kitchen table and sat across from her. "Integrating, I mean."

Fork in hand, she considered. One of the things I liked about my mom was how seriously she took what other people asked or said. She really listened, didn't just give you a blow-off answer.

"The closest I can come," she said, "is what it's like when you suddenly understand something. It just clicks into place. Right away, it fits into what you already know." She set her fork down. "Dr. Sam says it's like putting a jigsaw puzzle together. Instead of

71

pieces jumbled inside the box, now I can start seeing the complete picture. But the pieces are still themselves, too, even though they're together." She smiled. "Dr. Sam likes analogies. She uses them a lot."

Must be a shrink thing. Viking Clone's car analogy—

Wait. Dr. Sam.

Tiffany's voice through the intercom. "In Dr. Sam's office?"

Viking Clone, talking about Mom's new shrink. "You have no idea how fortunate your family is that Dr. Samuelson moved here—"

Dr. Samuelson was Dr. Sam.

Aha. One of the missiles hit home, and I absorbed the impact. Dr. Sam was Mom's new shrink. She specialized in DID. She must be Tara's shrink, too, since Tara left her jacket in that office. Which meant I'd been right in the first place.

Tara had DID.

For a second, I almost lost my appetite. So much for Tara just being shy. That had been what you'd call wishful thinking.

Mom had gone quiet. I jerked my attention back, but she was just eating her salad and looking thoughtful. My pulling away like that hadn't triggered anything the way it usually did.

I loaded my fork. "I've never heard you call her Dr. Sam before. You always use her whole name. Dr. Samuelson."

"Oh, that was because of Serena. She doesn't like nicknames."

That made sense. Serena was the alter who always called me Bancroft. "But she's okay with it now?"

Mom smiled. "She's one of the five who went in today."

"Oh." So once you integrated, you didn't get to make the rules anymore? I forked in a mouthful and chewed. I knew the answer to my next question, but I wanted to make sure. "Where's Dr. Sam's office?"

"The same place you go. The Dorst building. I call it The Doors, because even after I get inside, I have to go through so many of them before I get to see Dr. Sam."

72

The Doors. I liked that. "They have a lot of rules, too," I said.

"They do." She nodded seriously.

Nothing like sharing a warm mother/son moment about your shrinks' office building.

We ate in silence for a while.

"Why do you think it happened?" I asked. "You integrating, I mean?"

"I'm not sure. Some things Dr. Sam said last week…" Mom looked down at her left hand. "I've been thinking about them. That's what I was doing this afternoon, just sitting here thinking and drawing, when these five came together and told me they were going inside for good. It didn't even surprise me. Not really. It felt right."

I'd always known integration was the goal, but the principle still confused me. I knew in my head that the different alters weren't really separate people, but they all seemed so distinct. Mom and I could be watching a movie in the family room, and I'd look over just as somebody else came out to see what was on the screen. Sometimes I didn't even know what had made me look. Other times, it was something small but definite.

For instance.

All the little ones breathed faster than Mom. Hide held herself so still you could hardly tell she was breathing at all, while Me had an annoying habit of sighing heavily every few minutes.

Wait usually sat cross-legged. Libby liked to sort of curl up. Fighter never sat.

Cry squinted because she needed glasses, which amazed the optometrist who was in the middle of testing Mom's eyes when Cry pushed her way out. He said her eyes actually changed then. Cry didn't get the glasses, though, since she didn't come out very often. Nobody else wanted to carry them around all the time just for her.

Clarity came out even less than Cry. Her job was to pop out and check Dad's face, or mine, for clues on how to react to something new or confusing. You had to look fast if you wanted to see her in action.

73

"Who went in?" I asked. "Anyone I know?"

"Serena. And Watchful, Hope, Trying, and Libby."

"Libby?" The last bite of lasagna fell off my fork onto the table. I scooped it up. "Libby's gone? And Hope?" Hope came out whenever somebody was sick or in pain so she could take care of us. For such a little kid, she was good at it.

"Not *gone*, Bank. I told you. They just won't be out by themselves anymore. Now they'll be part of the person you see almost all the time. Me. That is, me, Meredith."

Having an alter named Me popping in and out had made for a lot of confusion over the years. Mom and I had joked that it was a good thing she didn't have another one named You. *Who did that? Me? No, You.*

I could tell I hadn't reacted so great. "I'm sorry, Mom. This is really hard for me to understand."

"I know, Bank." She took our dishes to the sink, then came back with a sponge to wipe up the cheesy mess I'd made on the table. "You've never known anything else. I suppose for you at first it *will* feel as if they've gone away."

"You don't seem different. You still seem like you."

"Think about yourself, Bank. What happened to the baby you used to be? Where did he go? And the toddler? Where did the ten-year-old go when you turned eleven?"

I'd never thought about that.

"They're still inside you," she said. "Part of you. They affect everything you do. But they don't suddenly come out and take over."

"Yeah, I guess that's true." I had a question for her, too, but I didn't want to ask it. Not yet. Instead, I said, "Does Dad know? About you integrating?"

She shook her head, eyes bright. "Don't say anything if you see him first. I'm so excited about telling him. This is what he's been waiting for." She smiled. "Five down, sixteen to go."

"Well, congratulations." I got up and poured myself a glass of juice, then snagged a handful of cookies. "Guess I better get

74

started on my homework."

First, though, I checked my email. Priorities.

Nothing from Jeff. Either the Minnesota winter had frozen his fingers, or his romantic life had heated up. Whatever, it came at a bad time for me, considering he was now my only friend. I started a new message.

To: jeffers@moondog.com
From: bankrobber@cvc.org
Subject:

Hey Jefferson. Nice to see you're friends with ☹ and ☺ now. Way to go. But it's time to say bye-bye to them and start writing words again.

Big news. My mom just had her first integration. 5 alters. It's a big deal and means she's really on the way. I've never seen her so chuffed. Viking Clone says this new shrink she's going to is good. That's double important because I just figured out that a girl at school has DID and goes to the same shrink. I hope Dr Sam can help this girl too because she's way too pretty to

I broke off and sat back to look at what I'd written.

Pretty, beautiful, gorgeous. Pulchritudinous. That's what I kept calling Tara, and it was true.

But North High had plenty of pretty girls. Maybe more than the national average. I noticed them, sure, but only because they *were* pretty. With Tara, there was something else. Something underneath her looks. Something I couldn't describe, much less name. She probably tried to keep it covered so people couldn't hurt her again, protecting herself until she got strong enough.

When Tara integrated someday, I had a feeling the person

we'd see wouldn't be the confident supermodel. It would be a girl more like the way Jeff described his brown-haired Rose.

I leaned forward and deleted the word *to*, then typed:

and sweet to waste years going through what Mom did. Viking Clone says DID has 70% complete recovery. They keep learning more about how to treat it so maybe this girl can

Babbling. I was babbling. Trying to write to Jeff while a daydream came out of nowhere and took over my mind.

Tara, healed and happy, though she would always be fragile from whatever broke her in the first place. Seeing my sensitivity, falling in love with it. And with the rest of me. I could see us marrying young, right out of high school. We'd go to college, walk around campus holding hands, study together in the evenings in our apartment, with me encouraging and protecting her. She'd look up at me with those big green eyes and...

Wow. I shook my head. Jeff and Rob must be rubbing off on me. I was getting as goofy as both of them, even using the word *sweet*. And *sensitivity*.

I turned back to the computer. This time I deleted everything after the part about Mom. Then I stared at the unfinished email without really seeing it.

Tara's jacket.

Should I call and tell her I had it, see if she wanted me to take it to her tonight? I didn't know her phone number, or anybody who did. And how would I explain why I had the jacket? What if she'd already called The Doors, and Tiffany told her that her good friend Bank Jonsson took it?

Tara probably didn't even know my name. She'd think I was a weirdo. She'd think I was stalking her. She'd call the police and get a restraining order on me.

"Oh, cripes," I muttered.

What an idiot I'd been today. When I saw Tara coming down the sidewalk toward me, I should've just kept walking. Tossed off a casual "How you doing?" and headed for my car. I had a right to be there.

What a complete and absolute idiot. And then, piling one bad choice on top of another, I'd gotten myself stuck with her jacket.

I bent over the keyboard again.

Mom told me a while ago she's looking forward to complete integration so she can finally watch a movie all the way through. She keeps missing important parts when somebody else gets interested and comes out to watch.

Hey, new word. Exoduster. It means a person who leaves in a hurry, like I did today to escape a killer Volvo. Tell you about it sometime.

Gotta go study. Hope you're busy saving your money for a phone. Get one with a camera and send me a picture of Rose.

Later $

There. That should be good motivation.

14

Fluke

Getting out of the shower the next morning, I skidded on the wet tiles and whacked my shin on the toilet.

"Figures," I muttered, clutching my leg. I'd already decided today would be the kind of day you wished you could just flush down the toilet. This confirmed it.

With no friends left, I had nobody to come and visit me in jail when Tara called the police on me for stalking her and stealing her jacket. And if life at home went anything like last night, my parents would be too busy staring soppily into each other's eyes to notice I was gone, much less post bail.

Mom was right. Dad had waited a long time for the alters to start going in for good. *He* sure wouldn't miss Libby. He didn't care about anyone except Meredith.

I was hyper-careful on the drive to school. The last thing I needed was to get stopped for some infraction and have the cop find a girl's leather jacket in my car. Stolen, obviously. I parked in the school lot and got out, rolling it up as small as I could, hoping nobody would recognize it and ask what I was doing with Tara's jacket.

That was crazy. The only reason I'd known the jacket was hers when I saw it in Dr. Sam's hand was because I'd just seen Tara coming from that side of The Doors. No one here would even notice.

When I walked into school, the first thing I did was trip over my shoelace. Nobody noticed that either. At least, I didn't hear howls of laughter. Dumping my book bag and Tara's jacket on the bench outside the office, I leaned against the wall and bent to tie my shoe.

"So *that*'s where I left it."

I froze, head down, fingers tangled in my shoelace. I'd have known that pretty southern voice anywhere.

"I was afraid I'd lost it for good. I love this jacket." Tara scooped it up from the bench and went down the hall talking to Lisa. Shiny black hair swinging, her perfect figure hidden by the bulky coat she'd worn today.

I stared after her. I couldn't believe it. There was no way this could have gone better.

Maybe I should send Jeff an email that just said ☺!

After that, the day went more like the first part of the week. Nobody to talk to, peanut butter sandwiches in the computer lab, trying not to notice Lovejoy crutching down the hall or Rob ignoring me. Life as usual.

Except that Jeff finally sent me a decent email.

To: bankrobber@cvc.org
From: jeffers@moondog.com
Subject:

Dude! As Kevin would say. That's so great about your mom. Do you think it's because of this new doc? What does your dad think? About the integration I mean. Is it weird for you that you won't see them again? Sweetie was always my favorite. Is she still around?

Sorry about ☺☹. I won't do it again.

Is there a way to make a rose?

J.

I'd completely forgotten about Sweetie. She always used to come out around Jeff, but only if I wasn't there. After our kindergarten Valentine party, I'd given her a heart-shaped candy with "Sweetie Pie" stamped on it, thinking she'd like it. Instead, the words terrified her. She decided I must be a cannibal who wanted to bake her in a pie and eat her. I hadn't seen her since.

Setting my peanut butter sandwich aside, I typed:

To: jeffers@moondog.com
From: bankrobber@cvc.org
Subject:

Hey Jefferson. I guess Sweetie's still around but Libby went in. Yeah, it's kind of sad, though Mom says they're not really gone. She says it's better because everything about them is here all the time instead of just coming out sometimes. I just can't get it. I guess it's kind of like if you'd moved to Minneapolis when you were 5 and moved back here now. You'd still be Jeff and I'd still be Bank but

Never mind. I don't know if I'll ever get it.

Yeah, Dad's really really happy. They keep looking at each other and just laughing. I've never seen him like that.

Sorry. No roses. I guess you could do @ and pretend it's a rosebud. You know how they kind of wrap around like that.

I stuck a ☺ on the end of the last sentence, then took it off. I didn't want to get Jeff started on them again.

A lot of kids griped about P.E. Including me. At least you got to run around instead of just sitting, but that was the only good thing I had to say about it.

Today we had badminton again, which I'd never liked. I always felt like an idiot, dancing around waving that skinny little racquet. And when you hit the birdie, even if you really whacked it, it just made a pathetic little *doink* sound.

After everybody trickled out of the locker room and lined up for roll call, Coach Summers divided us into teams for badminton doubles. He'd just gotten to me when Tom Lentmore, a senior who was captain of the tennis team, ran up.

"Hey, Coach," he said. "Can I borrow somebody?"

"Who?" Coach scowled at a kid who'd sneaked into line late and was trying to act like he'd always been there. "What for?"

"I've got three guys doing late tryouts for the tennis team. I need one more so I can watch them play doubles. It'll probably take the rest of the hour."

"You can have him." Coach jerked his thumb at me. "Go help them out, Bank."

"I've never played tennis before."

Tom was already moving, obviously in a hurry. He stopped, but Coach had turned away to yell at a couple of guys having a swordfight with their badminton racquets.

"Never? Seriously? Oh, well." Tom waved me to follow. "We'll switch you around with the different guys. Mostly I just need a body in the right spot so the guy on that team has somebody to play off. To position himself, you know."

I didn't know. Dropping my racquet onto the pile, I trotted after him. At least this got me out of badminton.

Tom headed for a door at the side of the gym. I knew the courts were outdoors, which meant we were in for a cold forty-five minutes or so, but he just had on shorts and a tee shirt. Those tennis guys must be tough.

He opened the door. Instead of gray skies and bone-chilling breezes, I was looking into a big, square room tacked onto the outside wall of the gym. Two tennis courts filled the space.

Tom saw me staring and grinned. "Nice, huh? We call it the courtroom. Some guy who made it big after high school donated this. He played tennis when he was here, and I guess he got sick of practicing in sixty-mile-an-hour winds. Wanted to make life better for the next generations."

He plucked a couple of tennis racquets off a bench. "We're happy about it. We kiss his foot every time we use these courts."

"What?"

Handing me a racquet, he pointed the other at a bronze plaque set into the wall by the door. It read *Ed Winton, 1972*. On it was what looked like a real tennis shoe, cut in half and coated with bronze. On a shelf underneath sat a creepy-looking little doll head with a yellow ponytail.

"Tennis Barbie." Tom picked up the head. "The guys kept taking her clothes off, so Coach tossed the body." He pushed the doll's face against the bronze shoe, made a kissing noise with his mouth, and set the head back on the shelf. "Thanks, Ed."

Three guys knocking a ball back and forth stopped to watch while Tom showed me how to hold the racquet.

"Go ahead and swing at anything that comes to you," he told me. "But don't run over and get in your partner's way. And don't break your wrist."

I just looked at him, offended. As if I planned to do either one.

He laughed. "I mean, don't bend your wrist when you hit the

ball. Like this." He showed me. "That's breaking your wrist. You do that in badminton, but not tennis. Keep it stiff."

Trevor, my so-called partner for the first round, was a junior I'd seen in the halls but didn't really know. The other two guys, Max and Rajid, I recognized from third-hour math. They all acted nice about it, but I could tell they weren't happy about playing with someone who didn't even know how to hold the racquet.

I didn't blame them. In their place, I'd already be feeling a lot of pressure about trying out for the team. This would just make it harder.

"Why don't you get someone else from the tennis team?" I asked Tom. "Instead of me, I mean."

He shrugged. "All the jocks have sixth-hour P.E. No one else is around till then, and this was the only time these guys could do it."

Clutching the racquet, I shuffled onto the court, wishing Coach had picked somebody else. I might not like badminton, but at least I knew how to play.

Sure enough, I missed everything that came my way—and they hit a lot more to me than I thought they would. I felt ridiculous, especially once when I swung so hard I spun all the way around like a demented ballerina. Everybody laughed, and a hot flick of anger shot up. Were they *trying* to make me look stupid? It sure seemed like it.

After what felt like an hour but was probably more like five minutes, as I was thinking how much I wanted to throw my racquet down and stomp off, Max sliced the ball straight at me. I saw the smirk on his face. Showing off, having fun at my expense.

This time, I didn't think about trying to hit the ball. I just stepped into it and swung. The racquet connected with a satisfying *whack*.

The ball zoomed about two inches above the net and whizzed between the two guys, landing just inside the back line and shooting toward the wall. All five of us watched it hit and bounce back. My hand vibrated and burned from the impact, but I felt great. I felt *great.*

"Wow!" Tom grinned. "Can you do that again?"

"I don't know. I can try."

He shook his head. "Don't try. Just do it."

Over the next half hour, I did it a lot of times. I also missed plenty, and some of the balls I hit took off at weird and obviously illegal angles. One torpedoed sideways and would've knocked Trevor's head off if he hadn't dropped to the floor. Everybody laughed, but this time so did I. And all three of them made some wild shots, too.

They did most of the playing and all the serving, since they were the ones trying out for the team. But now we looked more like a real doubles game. Not so lopsided.

At first it was like my body knew what to do, and my mind just got in the way. But after a while, things pulled together, and more of my shots went where I wanted them. Tom had me trade around to partner with Max and then Rajid. I got better each time.

Afterwards, the five of us headed for the locker room. Tom was ahead, talking to Trevor, but then they dropped back to walk on either side of me.

"You told me you never played before," Tom said. "Is that true, or did you just mean it had been a while?"

"It's true. I used to watch tennis on TV, but I never played." I grinned. "Couldn't you tell?"

"Actually, no. That was amazing, Bank. You've *never* played before?"

I shook my head.

"Well, you're a natural. You need coaching, and lots of work, but you could be good. You have the instincts of a first-class fuzzhead."

Max caught up with us. "That was your first time? For real?"

Did I look like a liar or something? "Yup."

Max stared at Rajid, then back at me. "Once you started hitting, we thought you'd just been goofing off at first. Pretending you never even held a tennis racquet." He did an exaggerated imitation of me, sticking his racquet out and staring at it like he was afraid it would bite him. Then he dropped the pose. "Seriously."

"He's a natural. I know guys who'd kill to have that backhand." Tom slapped my shoulder. "You interested in playing some more?"

We'd reached the locker room. Everybody stopped and looked at me.

"What do you mean?"

"Practice some during the week. Get some unofficial coaching." He looked at the others. "What do you guys think?"

"Sure," Trevor said. Max and Rajid nodded.

Tom turned back to me. "We could see how you shape up. You interested?"

"Yeah. Yeah, that'd be great."

Everyone else from my P.E. class had already left. In the locker room, I shifted into exoduster mode, pulling jeans and sweatshirt over my gym clothes without showering. The girl who sat next to me in biology would probably tell Lovejoy how much I stunk. Then Lovejoy would say she already knew that.

But I didn't care.

I was *chuffed*.

15

Unfluke

That night, I dreamed about fuzzy green balls bouncing and racquets swishing through the air. I woke up with my legs twitching as if they'd been trying to run.

When I rolled out of bed, I let out a grunt of pained surprise. My legs ached. So did my right arm, as I discovered when I got in the shower and reached to pull the glass door shut. I stood under the spray of hot water, letting it beat against my sore muscles. They weren't used to working that hard.

I bent over and massaged my calves. "Come on, guys, quit complaining. You know it was worth it."

As I left the house, I got another surprise. This was a good one, though.

In middle or late January, Oklahoma always gets a few days of fake spring, sunny and warm enough to fool trees and bushes into budding out just in time to get blasted again. This morning, it felt like we'd jumped straight into June. I didn't need my sweatshirt, much less the heavy jacket I'd been wearing all month.

"All *right!*" I peeled off the jacket and tossed it onto the back seat. Pushing up my sleeves, I slid into the car and opened the windows. Our fake spring never lasted long, but I would enjoy it while it did. And today was Friday, so it should last at least through the weekend.

On my way to second-hour computer lab, Trevor stopped me in the hall.

"Hey, Bank, what do you think?" He waved a hand toward

the window, where sunshine cut through the usual gloom of low-watt artificial lights. "Want to hit some balls after school? I got an outdoor court reserved."

"Sure." Then I hesitated. Max and Rajid had played great yesterday, but Trevor's game was amazing. "Look, this is really nice of you. Coaching me, I mean. I know it won't be as much fun for you as playing somebody else."

"No, it's cool. There's a couple of freshmen who want to get some practice, too. See if they might be up for joining the team next year. This'll be more of a mix."

"That's great." I just hoped they wouldn't blow me off the court.

"Okay, good. See you there." He glanced at my jeans and Nikes. "What you've got on should be okay for what we're doing today. But if you want your P.E. gear, just be sure to get it before they lock up the gym. You sore today?"

I nodded.

"You really went after it yesterday." He grinned. "This time, we'll do some stretching first."

When Max and Rajid walked into math class, I waved from my seat in the back corner. Just being friendly. I didn't expect them to come over. But Max said something to Rajid, who nodded, and they headed my way. Max sat next to me, and Rajid slid sideways into the seat in front of him.

"How's the arm today?" Rajid asked.

"It's okay. Kind of sore."

"Wow." Max made an imaginary telescope with his hands and pretended to peer at my feet through it. I had my desk scooted against the back wall, with my legs stretched out full length. He squinted. "How tall are you, anyway?"

"Six four."

He whistled. "You know, that kind of height's good for tennis. It's hard for your opponent to hit over your head, and you can cover more area with your arms."

"And legs." Rajid poked him in the knee. They both grinned.

"I'm slow." Max shrugged. "I'm good enough hitting to make up for it some, at this level anyway. But I just can't run fast enough. I could never turn pro."

I sure hadn't noticed him being slow.

The bell sounded. As Mrs. Adams swept the room with her death-ray glare, everybody faced forward and shut up. I saw Rob's head just turning away. Had he been watching us?

All I could see of Kevin was the hump of his skinny back. He must be digging in his book bag, trying to find his math book in the usual mess of crumpled papers and rotting food. By the end of semester, his pack would've morphed into a combination science experiment and city dump. I saw him pull the book out and turn triumphantly toward Rob, peeling an ice cream wrapper off the cover.

Kevin was a mess. But I kind of missed being around him.

I went to lunch with Max and Rajid and sat with their friends on the opposite side of the cafeteria from Alex's group. We mostly talked about tennis. When Max told about yesterday's doubles tryout, including Trevor's swan dive onto the floor, my face prickled with hot embarrassment. Mostly because the way he described it made me sound way better than I really was.

"So, we're thinking this guy's a puffball," Max said. "And Raj and I are just standing there waiting for him to miss again, when he burns the ball just above the net and right between us."

He shot his fist through the air, almost knocking the hamburger out of Rajid's hand. "*Zip!* All you can see is this blur. Then it ricochets off the back wall like a bomb, and we're all ducking and running for our lives."

Everybody was laughing. Max didn't mind using exaggeration to get his audience going, and he was good at it. Rajid and I laughed, too, and we'd been there.

The three of us left the cafeteria together. Max turned off into his Latin class, then stuck his head back out and said, "Raj, you still up for some tennis tomorrow afternoon? My place?"

Rajid nodded and looked at me.

Max grinned. "You want to come, too?"

"Sure. If you really want me."

As a couple of girls tried to squeeze past him into the room, Max clasped his hands over his heart and warbled, "Oh, we wa-a-ant you."

Rajid sighed. "Come on, Bank."

"Where're you headed?"

"English." He looked at me. "We're in the same class."

"Oh." I felt stupid.

He smiled. "Without Max, I'm so quiet nobody notices me." As we climbed the stairs, he said, "Max can be a little over the top. But he's a good guy."

I nodded. Several times today, Max had reminded me of Kevin. With a few extra IQ points.

Going out to the court after school, I was tempted to come up with an excuse to back out. Yesterday must've been a fluke. Like when an amateur bowler has one of those amazing games where he throws all strikes and spares, or a loser football team destroys the champions who'd expected to walk all over them. Sometimes that happens. Yesterday it had happened to me. I didn't want to see the look on Trevor's face when I swatted air and tripped over my Nikes.

Oh, well. If I put it off today, it would just be worse tomorrow.

Trevor and I lined up against the two freshmen, Eric and Tony. I wasn't sure which was which, since I'd been too jittery to pay attention when Trevor introduced them. Not big guys, but they both looked strong and confident.

"Let's warm up first," Trevor said. "We can work on your service later, Bank, and then we'll play a set. Right now, let's just rally. That means just hit it back and forth."

Eric and Tony looked at each other and snickered. I could tell they couldn't believe their luck. One of their opponents was so green, the other had to explain everything.

My hands actually shook while I waited for Trevor to get things started. I kept telling myself this was no big deal, that he knew it was only my second time to even pick up a racquet. Let Eric and Tony laugh all they wanted. It didn't matter. This wasn't even a real game.

Trevor dropped the ball and hit it on the bounce. It sloped over the net, an easy warm-up shot, and Eric/Tony had no trouble getting to it.

When he popped it back to me, there was no doubt in my mind I'd miss. The only question was, would I also fall down? I swung.

Thwack!

The ball skimmed over the net and touched down about a foot inside the back line. Eric and Tony spun around to watch it smash into the tall wire fence behind them. I heard the metallic clatter just as Trevor shouted, "Good!"

When I glanced at him, he grinned and gave me a thumbs up.

As the ball rolled back onto the court, E/T scooped it up with his racquet. "Hey," he said. "I thought we were just going to warm up first."

"Yeah, that's true." Trevor shot me a fake stern look. "Take it easy on these kids, Bank. Okay?"

"Sorry."

One of life's beautiful moments.

We played for an hour and a half. By the time we quit, the sky held just enough light to make you think it was day, but at ground level it was getting hard to see the ball coming. Today might feel like June, but this was still January. Sunset came early.

"Okay, that's game," Trevor called. He picked up the ball bag he'd dropped next to the net. "Let's close it down while we can still see to get our stuff."

Eric and Tony had won the last couple of games, coming up from behind. They were psyched. "Let's finish the set. We can use

90

the lights."

"School has 'em locked. They don't want kids here after dark unless it's an official match." Trevor zipped the cover over his racquet. "Two years ago, some waffleheads climbed the fence to play and left the lights on all night. Big energy burn. School board was ready to close down the whole tennis program. If The Bee wasn't a major fan, we'd be history."

He headed for the fence, and I went to help him collect balls.

"Wafflehead?" I heard one E/T say to the other. "What's a wafflehead?"

When we had everything, Trevor shut the gate behind us and shook it to make sure the lock had caught. E/T took off, racing each other to the parking lot.

"You can hang onto that racquet for now," Trevor said. "When you're ready to buy one, talk to me first. I'll help you get a good one."

"Thanks."

"Next time, let's work on your serve. That's the weakest part of your game."

I nodded. "I know. I just can't get it."

"Don't worry. It'll come." He pointed. "Lights are on in the gym. I'm going to see if I can still get in."

I was in no hurry to leave. I dropped onto a bench facing the courts and watched darkness spread. Soon I could barely see the pale line of net stretching across the tennis court. Every part of me felt tired and sore and hungry—and happier than I'd been in my life. I wasn't ready to enter any tournaments yet, but even to me, it was obvious Tom had been right. This was where I belonged.

As I leaned back, my hands resting on Trevor's racquet, two questions rolled up from the back of my mind.

Trevor had been a huge help. He was a great player and knew a lot about the tennis program. This made his third year at North. So why was he just now trying out for the team?

The second question had more to do with the dark, balmy

evening than with any part of reality.

If I made the tennis team, would Lovejoy Fox come and watch?

16

Fuzzhead

To: jeffers@moondog.com
From: bankrobber@cvc.org
Subject:

Hey Jefferson. You'll never guess. I'm now a jock. NOT BASKETBALL even though all my life that's what everybody kept saying I'd end up doing. I don't like games where you get tangled up in people and knock them down. That's not supposed to happen in this sport. Though the first time I played I did come close to knocking a guy's head off. He ducked.☺

Tennis! I'm now a fuzzhead. It's like I was made to do it. When the ball comes at me, somehow I just know what to do. Most of the time anyway. Tom Lentmore is captain of the tennis team and he thinks I could be a first class player. The amazing thing is I think so too.☺

Remember how we used to watch tennis on TV? Maybe all those hours are finally paying off.

Later $

I decided it should be safe to put in a couple of smiley faces without getting Jeff started on them again. He was too busy trying to come up with a better rose icon. His last letter had been all about his blue-eyed Rose, with so many @s scattered through the sentences, at first I thought he'd sent me a long list of email addresses. Not a big success.

As my words disappeared into cyberspace, I leaned back and thought about what I'd written. To anybody else, that last part would sound braggy. With Jeff, though, it was like telling your brother. You can tell family things you wouldn't say to anybody else.

I was now a fuzzhead.

Grinning, I bit into one of the chocolate chip cookies I'd scooped up from the kitchen after lunch. *A fuzzhead.*

At North, almost everybody was a something-head.

Tennis players were fuzzheads. Basketball players were highheads. Golfers were puttheads. Football players were pigheads, partly because footballs used to be made out of pigskin, but mostly because of the way some of those guys ate.

Baseball players had earned the name hardheads, since that's what it took to survive. North had never had a decent baseball team. Rumor had us holding the state record for number of players sent to the hospital each season, mostly beaned by wild throws or missed pop flies.

Outside of sports, the super-smart kids and computer nerds were hackerheads. Rockheads crouched on the opposite end of the intelligence scale. Conheads would probably end up in jail, potheads were druggies, and deadheads made up the drink-and-drive group. Kevin started calling that last group noheads after one guy drove in front of a train, but that was just too gross for anybody else. Deadheads sounded bad enough.

Not everybody used the labels. A lot of kids didn't. I hardly ever did, probably for the same reason I didn't like the sub-language of email and texting. Fuzzhead sounded pretty good, though, now that I was one.

But what was a waff:ehead?

I took another bite. Last night, when Trevor told us about the kids who'd left the lights on, he called them waffleheads. I'd never heard that one before. E/T obviously hadn't either. I should ask Rob—

The thought had rolled into my head before I could stop it. The cookie sagged into bitter mush in my mouth. After I swallowed it, my stomach felt jumpy.

Every day as I'd driven to school since the Bank-being-a-jerk disaster, I'd braced myself to run into Rob and Kevin in the halls and cafeteria without letting it bother me. I'd done a good job of that. The old friendships were dead. Even if Rob and Mandy broke up, and the reason for our split went away, I could never see Rob as a real friend. Or Kevin, for going along with him.

A friend didn't drop you just because you did something stupid.

I brushed crumbs off my mouse pad. Jeff had given it to me the day he moved away, an early birthday present since he wouldn't be here for the real thing. While I was outside saying good-bye to the rest of his family, he put it on my desk and changed my screen saver to *Happy Birthday Bro*. I found it after they drove off.

No card. It didn't need one.

Solid and simple, the printed words on the mouse pad read, *There is a friend who sticks closer than a brother. Proverbs 18:24.*

The sick feeling had faded. I took a deep breath and reached for another cookie, glancing at the clock by my bed. One-fifteen. Almost time to go meet the guys at Max's apartment complex and play some tennis at the courts there. Anxiety flicked, but not nearly as strong as yesterday. I hadn't made an idiot of myself with Trevor then, and I wouldn't today.

I was a fuzzhead. Not a fluke.

Trevor's tennis racquet lay on my extra bed. I picked it up and swung it a couple of times. I'd have to ask Max and Rajid if they knew what a wafflehead was. Probably North High tennis slang, but for what? Maybe a player who was so bad, he kept missing the ball and hitting himself in the face. A racquet could leave marks that looked like a waffle.

Sort of, anyway.

As I stuffed the last cookie into my mouth, my cell phone rang. "Oh, cripes," I mumbled, digging in the pocket of my sweat pants. "I've *got* to change that." Rudolph and his megawatt nose were definitely getting on my nerves.

I glanced at the caller ID. Max.

He must be calling to cancel. I should've realized he just wanted to play with Rajid. He hadn't included me until it obviously would have been rude not to. I should've picked up on that and said I was busy or something.

Or something.

I sagged onto the bed, letting the racquet drop to the floor. "Hey, Max." I tried to sound like a guy whose schedule was so crammed with fun activities, canceling would be no problem. I sounded more like a pathetic loser whose mouth was so crammed with cookie, I'd just sprayed soggy crumbs all over my yellow tee shirt. I swiped at them, leaving chocolate smears. *Great.*

"Bank? That you?"

I swallowed. "Yuh. S'me."

"You on the road yet?" The sound of people whacking tennis balls came through the line, along with cheering and laughter. Good times, good company.

"Nope. Still home."

"Good. Whoa, great shot!" he said. "Anyway, we gotta make a change."

I knew it. "Sure. No problem. I'm—"

"A whole crowd's already got both courts here. I asked, and they're doing one of those round robin tournaments. They'll be here all afternoon."

Max whistled, and I jerked the phone away from my head. "Wow, this old guy's really good," he said. "Anyway, I called Raj.

He lives over by Cunningham, so he checked and said there's one court free. It's not in great shape, but it's better than nothing. You know where that is?"

"Cunningham Park? Sure."

"I'm gonna leave now and go rally some with Raj so nobody grabs his court. With this kind of weather, everybody and their grandma's out. Hey, you got a racquet?"

"Trevor loaned me one."

"Trev did? No joke?" He whistled again, but I heard it coming and got the phone away in time. "That guy *never* loans his stuff out. He must think you're good or something."

"No, it was just, you know, he knew I needed one and—"

"Sure." Max laughed. "See you in a few."

Shoving the phone back into my pocket, I got a surge of happiness so strong it scared me. I took a deep breath and stood up, gripping Trevor's racquet in both hands. "Can Bankie come out and play?" I said, making fun of myself.

Mom must be right. The little-kid me was still in there somewhere. So chuffed about making a new friend, I was practically hyperventilating.

I guess that's something you never outgrow.

17

Wafflehead

The net sagged, cracks zigzagged across the concrete, and the painted lines had faded into near invisibility. But we had a great time. We played two against one, with Max and Rajid trading off as my partner. When we switched to one-on-one, whoever wasn't playing coached me from the sidelines.

That's when I figured out the serve. Actually, I didn't figure it out. On the second game, it just fell into place. *Whack!*

I won against Max that game, and it annoyed me. I didn't like him going easy on me because I was a beginner.

"You shouldn't have let me win," I said as we walked off.

"*Let* you win! You gotta be joking." Max grabbed a towel and wiped his face. "You ran me into the ground."

Rajid, usually so quiet, was whooping and jumping up and down on the far side. He ran over to us.

"No mercy!" he shouted, grinning. "You should never have told him you're a slow runner, Max. He *used* that against you."

I hadn't thought about it, but that's exactly what I'd done. Once my serve started going where I wanted, Max had to dive for it. That meant his returns got less controlled and easier for me to nail. I could zing the ball to the far corners so he had to run for it each time.

My annoyance morphed into guilt. "Wow, Max. I didn't…look, I'm really—"

"Lucky for you I'm a good loser. Now *murder* him, Raj." Max waved the towel at Rajid and staggered to the bench, faking exhaustion.

Rajid didn't murder me, but he did win. Next game, Max beat me, too. But they both had to work at it.

We played on Sunday after church and Monday after school. Trevor joined us on Tuesday, which made things even better. All three of them had made the team, and they talked about getting me in shape for trying out.

"Man, that would have to be some kind of record," Max said as we got our things together to head home. "Guy picks up a racquet for the first time in his life. Two months later, he makes the team and wipes out the competition. National headlines!"

"I don't think so," I mumbled.

"That'd be great." Trevor reached for his racquet cover. "But I don't think so either. You need a lot of work, Bank. You'll have to wait for next year to make the team." He zipped his racquet in. "Tomorrow? Got to take advantage of this weather."

"Sure." Then I remembered. "Oh, cripes."

"What's the matter?"

Tomorrow was Wednesday. Viking Clone. "I've got this appointment. Right after school."

Nobody asked, "What kind of appointment?" or anything nosy like that. But my face prickled with embarrassment, and I knew it had gone red. For the first time since Tom had pulled me out of badminton and into tennis, I felt my arms and legs stretching into cooked noodle configuration.

Just before the silence became too awkward, Max drawled, "So-o-o." He pulled the visor of his ball cap down over his eyes. "What's her name?"

Trevor popped him on the back with his racquet, then used it to point. "Go find that ball in the grass over there. It's mine, but you're the wafflehead who lobbed it over the fence."

Max made a face. "I hate that stuff. It won't die in the winter like normal grass. It just goes stiff and stabs you." But he turned and ambled cheerfully away. Rajid went with him.

My various appendages shrank thankfully back to their

normal dimensions. I took a deep breath. "Trevor. What's a wafflehead?"

"Wafflehead? Oh, I don't know. Goofy, no-brain. That kind of thing."

"Where's it come from? I thought I'd heard all the head words."

"No, it's just a family thing." He laughed. "My sister threw a waffle at my little brother, and it hit him on the head and stuck. Syrup, you know. Tess's boyfriend was over, and Tim kept trying to embarrass her in front of him. I don't remember what he said, but it must've been pretty bad. She didn't even get in trouble for throwing the waffle."

He grinned. "They're married now. Ben says he's extra nice to her whenever they have waffles."

I didn't realize I was staring until he shrugged and said, "Guess you had to be there." He turned away and yelled, "Max! More to your right."

Driving home, I kept thinking about Trevor's story. I could picture the whole scene as clearly as if I'd seen it in a movie. The sister, the boyfriend, the obnoxious little brother. The waffle flipping through the air to plaster itself against the kid's head. A moment of shocked silence. Then the room loud with laughter as syrup drips down his face. A funny family story, the kind that turns into a family legend.

My family had no stories like that. None.

When I got home, I heard the thin, whimpery sobs of one of the little ones. I tracked the sound to the family room. As I walked in, Mom gasped and shrank back.

"Sorry," I said quickly. "I should've called out."

She gazed at me with big, watery eyes. "Bank. I'm so sad."

"Is this, um…" I always hated to guess who it was. Some of the alters got offended if I was wrong. She'd made herself as small as possible in a corner of the sofa, a pillow on her lap, and I heard her sigh. "Is this Me?" I asked.

"Um-hm."

I went over and sat on the floor in front of her. "What's the matter?"

"I'm scared."

"Why?"

Her voice went so soft and quivery, I had to lean forward to hear. "Some of the ones inside aren't doing their jobs. They won't come out when they're supposed to. It isn't *safe* anymore."

I figured she must be talking about the five who'd integrated. "They have different jobs now. Remember? Now their job is to be inside all the time. It's even safer than it used to be."

She stared at me.

"*You* know it isn't safe," she said. "You're sad, too."

I couldn't hide anything from my mom. Not from any of my moms.

"Yeah. I mean, it's safe. That's not the problem." I leaned back on my hands. "But, yeah, I'm kind of sad right now."

We both sighed heavily at the same time. I laughed, but she just frowned at me. Most of the alters, including Me, had zero sense of humor.

"I guess sometimes things don't feel as safe as they really are," I said. "You just have to believe it. Take it by faith. Come on." I stood. "Let's go make dinner before Dad gets home."

Since Me didn't know how to cook, she zipped inside and Mom came out. "Dinner's in the slow cooker. Tortilla soup." She uncurled and put her feet on the floor. "I was trying to listen, Bank, but I couldn't hear it all. What's wrong with Me?"

"She's scared. Things are changing, and it doesn't feel safe.

She says people inside aren't doing their jobs."

"I know." She looked down at the pillow on her lap. For the first time, I noticed a few white hairs among the dark brown. It startled me. Mom always seemed so much younger than her age. Maybe because so much of her was.

"Change is scary," she said. "Even when you know it's good." She looked up. "Bank, are you sorry I'm your mother?"

Guilt slammed me. It was almost like she'd been inside my head, as if she'd watched me thinking about Trevor's story and wishing our family was more normal. The same way she watched and listened when the other alters came out.

She hadn't. I knew that. But I also knew there was no point in telling her anything except the truth.

"No." I crouched in front of her. "I love you, Mom. But sometimes…well, I guess sometimes I wish our whole family was different. Including me."

I'd never said anything like that to her. I didn't think she could've taken it before. But things *were* changing.

She reached out to brush the hair back from my forehead. "I like who you are, Bank." Her gaze stayed on my face, serious and steady. "I think someday you will, too."

18

Shrinking

The more time passed, and the busier I got with tennis, the less I would think about Lovejoy.

At least, that's how I figured it would work.

But it didn't.

In the halls, part of me was always listening for her voice, watching for her to swing into sight on her crutches. Sometimes I heard her laughing before I saw her. She and Mandy especially had a great time together, but she had plenty of other friends.

Plenty. And I could never be part of that.

Whenever the thought shoved its way in, it felt like someone was blowing up a balloon inside my chest. The balloon would swell and stretch to the far edge of bursting, then quiver and shrink down again, thick and rubbery. Either way, it didn't leave much room for my lungs. Every day as I climbed the stairs to sixth-hour biology, where I knew I'd see Lovejoy, it wasn't just running all the way from the gym that had me breathless. I didn't puff like that when I played tennis.

This almost felt harder than having Jeff move away.

On Wednesday, I was leaving biology when Lovejoy's voice cut through the end-of-day hubbub. "Ba—"

I turned so fast, my left heel landed on my right toe. Kids around me hooted as I wobbled and barely caught my balance. The commotion drowned out what Lovejoy was saying, but I saw her wave at the girl who always sat next to me. The girl's name was Bambi, of all things, and she was one of Lovejoy's many friends.

Bambi. Not Bank. I lurched out through the doorway, banging my shoulder hard on the frame. More hoots and snickers.

"Oh, forget it," I muttered and headed down the stairs, rubbing my shoulder. Then, rounding the corner toward my locker, I almost crashed into Tara Prentiss. She slipped gracefully past without looking up.

I watched her go. Tara usually wore jeans, like most girls, but today she had on a short red skirt. I remembered the first day I'd seen her, and the way Rob had said, "You mean the girl with the great legs?" She really did have a supermodel figure. Better, probably, since no one had done any photoshopping here. Nothing about Tara needed help.

Not on the outside, anyway.

When I turned away, I saw a group of girls watching me and giggling. They must've seen me staring after Tara. My face prickled with embarrassment as I headed for my locker.

Nice of me to provide all this entertainment for the school.

On my way to The Doors, I decided I was getting in a rut. So instead of four cheeseburgers, I got four bacon cheeseburgers. Definite improvement.

As I pulled out into traffic again, I wondered if Tara was on her way to see Dr. Sam. Most people probably went the same time every week, like me. If I saw her after my appointment, like last time, I could offer her a ride for next week.

Yeah, right. I could just see myself doing that.

I glanced at the passenger seat, trying to imagine Tara sitting there. Laughing at something clever I'd said, or gazing seriously up at me with those amazing eyes. But then the eyes darkened to brown.

A pair of crutches had been tossed onto the back seat, and—

My foot slammed onto the brake. The Prizm shuddered to a squealing stop at the red light, its nose sliding into the crosswalk. I leaned back and blew out a long breath. *Keep your eyes on the road. Keep your mind on your driving.* Between Tara and Lovejoy, my mind had spent a lot of time lately on two girls who weren't even talking to me. One didn't know I was alive. The other probably wished I wasn't.

Oh, well. At least I had tennis. And tennis actually liked me back.

Going into The Doors, I looked up and waved at the security camera. It waggled at me. On my way through the receptionist's room, Tiffany patted the top of her head and called, "Your part's crooked."

I grinned back. "I don't *have* a part."

This time, when Viking Clone came out to the waiting room to get me, he couldn't quite carry off his usual neutral-but-receptive attitude.

"Whoa!" I halted in mid-rise, magazine in hand, then straightened. "Impressive."

It *was* impressive. Fantastic shades of green and purple, with one artistic red patch surrounding a thin line of scab on his cheekbone. In the very center, a tiny slit of eye gleamed through the puffiness.

"So, how'd you get the shiner?" I followed him into his sanctum. "Did one of your clients freak out and punch you?"

I wasn't joking. I really wanted to know. Maybe somebody else had taken Viking Clone's NBR attitude as a challenge. But instead of verbally surprising him out of it, which was my plan, they'd gone the more direct route. *Pow.*

Being a shrink might be even more interesting than I'd realized.

He closed the door. "This time isn't about me, Bank. Let's not waste it."

That really sounded like Dad. And it probably meant a client *had* punched him, or he would at least tell me the basics of what happened. Ran into a door, tripped over a rug, that sort of thing. Checking out the landscape over the desk, I caught a glint in the cows' eyes. Too bad they couldn't talk.

I dragged the only chair I hadn't tried yet into place. This one sat lower, with wooden arms and legs and plaid upholstery. It looked like something you'd find in a cheap furnished apartment.

Viking Clone picked up the Dr Pepper waiting on his desk and held it out. "Maybe today we'll actually talk about you."

"Um, thanks." I took the bottle and sat down. Way down. This definitely wasn't the chair for me. "What do you mean?"

He lowered himself into his chair. "Your first session, we talked about your mother. Last time, we talked about your classmate who might have DID." He raised his eyebrows, then winced and touched his bruised cheek. "So far, I haven't heard much about you."

I'd never heard that edge to his voice before. I looked at his hands.

Aha.

The left hand lay flat on his leg, but it didn't look relaxed. And when he dropped his right hand after touching his face, the fingers closed tightly over his left wrist. A bigger hint sat in plain sight on the desk beside him. A supersized bottle of aspirin.

Viking Clone still had one more appointment after me. He was hanging in there, but obviously tired and hurting. He deserved some cooperation.

"Okay," I said. "I know exactly why my dad wanted me to start counseling. He thinks it's been bad for me to have a mom with DID."

"What do *you* think about that?"

Shrink-talk. It could mean, did I think it had been bad for me to have a mom with DID? Or it could mean, what did I think about my dad thinking it had been bad for me to have a mom with DID? Since I hadn't really talked about Dad yet, I decided to go with the second option.

"I know it bothers him that it just seems normal to me." I opened my drink and watched it foam to the top. "I don't even remember when I figured out she was different from other kids' moms. As long as I can remember, I've watched out for her. Sort of protected her. I was always hyper-aware of what things meant. You know, like the look in her eye. Or when she does this."

I moved my left hand the way Mom always did when somebody else wanted to come out.

"It wasn't a conscious thing, you know. I just did it." I took a drink. The fizz felt good in my mouth.

"My friend Jeff says everybody does that. Like, when your dad walks into the room with a certain look on his face, you know it's *not* a good time to ask him for something." I grinned, thinking of Jeff's dad. You didn't have to do much guessing with him. Whatever he felt showed loud and clear.

"Jeff says what's different is that most kids figure out their parents so they can make it work for them. For the kid. You know, to keep from getting in trouble, or when and how to get what you want. But I was doing it for her. For my mom."

I looked at him. He nodded.

"So, anyway, a couple of years ago my dad started talking about role reversal. About me acting more like I'm the dad and Mom's the kid. He said it wasn't good. He said I should back off." I felt a flick of anger and pushed it down. It popped back up. "But what was I supposed to do? Just stand there and let things get bad?"

"How would things get bad?"

"How? Well, people…they didn't understand." I had sharp memories of that. "They'd stare, or laugh, or it would freak them out. They'd ask if she was crazy. One time at the mall when she got scared and hid under our table at the food court, somebody called the police. I thought *that* was crazy."

He watched me, one hand against his sore cheek.

"After Gatekeeper, things got better. Mom—Meredith—

mostly stayed out when she needed to look normal. I still didn't like having her come to school, though, like for parent/teacher conference. She did okay, but I was always afraid something might happen. Embarrass me." I gripped my Dr Pepper in both hands. "It hurt her feelings, even though she said she understood."

"How did you feel about that?"

"About hurting her? I hated it." I stared down at the bottle in my hands. "When I was a kid, we were at the park one time. One of the really young alters was out, playing on the swings. Some other kids came running up, and I tried to get her to leave before they got to us. She didn't want to stop. I got mad. I said…"

Blood pushed against the veins on each side of my forehead. I'd never told anybody about this. Even Jeff didn't know this part.

"I told her I didn't want anybody to see how *stupid* she was being. Meredith came out then, and we left." Watching my fingers turn the bottle around and around, I swallowed hard. "Next day when I got home from school, she didn't answer. I went in the kitchen, and the back door was open. I found her out in the yard. In the garden." I looked up. "She'd cut her throat."

Viking Clone was silent. His one eye looked sympathetic.

"Hope—that's one of the alters—had kept her from cutting deep enough to kill herself. But she must've kept trying. She had one long cut, all the way across, and lots of little ones. Blood all over her neck and hands. There were these little white flowers by her face, and they had red splotches on them." For some reason, that was the part I most hated remembering.

I tried to keep my eyes steady on his face. "It was my fault."

"You blame yourself for what she did?"

"It *was* my fault. It was because of what I said. I called her stupid. That's what those people, her foster parents, always said when she didn't do what they wanted. It was the worst thing you could say to her. And I knew it."

"You sound angry, Bank."

"Well, sure. It was a rotten thing to do."

108

"So you feel angry with yourself."

I nodded.

"Are you angry with her, too?"

"With Mom? For cutting herself? No. Why would—look, could we talk about something else?"

I stared down at my hands. Fists again.

"I'm sorry," I said. "I didn't mean to be rude. This was a mistake. I really don't want to talk about this right now."

If Viking Clone had been his normal self, he might have pushed it. I don't know. As it was, neutral-but-receptive looked more like here-but-wish-I-wasn't. His glance flicked from the aspirin bottle to the wall clock behind me. I checked the reflected minute hand. More than half an hour to go, and it looked like we'd both had all we could take. Even the cows sagged.

"Dr. Kind, we don't have to keep going. I mean, I'm okay if you want to, you know, stop early." I pointed at my eye.

"Thank you." His chair creaked as he shifted. "That's thoughtful of you, Bank."

Was that sarcasm? I studied his face, but the swollen eye made him more unreadable than ever.

"Let's finish out our time." He smiled faintly. "You choose the subject, Bank."

So I told him about Mom integrating, and about tennis and the guys I'd gotten to know because of it. Putting in plenty of details, I had no trouble filling up the time. It was actually kind of fun. How often does somebody just want to listen to you?

"So, yeah," I said, when my fifty minutes were up. "Things are going great."

I don't know why I said that. I never said that kind of thing.

Because throwing out a statement like that is like walking up to the school's biggest, meanest conhead, sticking out your chin, and saying, "Hey, you big idiot. Dare you to slug me."

You won't have long to wait.

19

Meltdown

I hadn't said anything to my parents about my first two sessions with Viking Clone, even though—or maybe because—I knew it killed Dad not to ask. But the black eye was just too good to keep to myself. I told them about it at dinner that night.

Mom set down her glass. "Yesterday Dr. Sam told me one of her associates got a black eye. That must have been Dr. Kind. She said a client hit him."

"Aha!" I thumped the table. "I thought so."

"Why?" Dad was actually smiling. For some reason, he seemed happier with me lately. Probably overflow from Mom's integration.

"Well, he has this sign on his door," I said. "It says if the therapist is more than five minutes late for your appointment, you're supposed to go tell the receptionist. It says, 'Do *not* knock on this door.' So I figured it means if he's late, it's because the guy before you freaked out. He doesn't want you making things worse by banging on the door." I grinned.

They both stared at me, expressions blank. I saw Clarity pop out, check Dad's face for clues about how Mom should react, then zip back in.

I sighed and scooped up a spoonful of rice. "*I* thought it was funny."

Mom smiled, indulging me.

Dad turned to her. "Why did Dr. Samuelson tell you? Seems rather unprofessional."

"We were talking about anger. She asked what kinds of things make me angry."

So. This must be the week for the Jonsson shrinks to poke around in our psyches, searching for hidden rage.

He set down his fork. "What did you tell her?"

I stopped chewing. That just wasn't the kind of question we ever asked. If Mom wanted to tell us, she would. But we never asked.

She answered steadily enough. "I told Dr. Sam I don't get angry. That's when she told me about the other therapist and the black eye. She said some people won't admit they're angry until it fills them so full they explode. She said that's what happened this time."

The tension around her eyes lightened. "Dr. Sam said she didn't want me punching her later, so I might as well go ahead and admit I get angry sometimes."

"Did you?" Dad asked.

"I did. But I don't want to talk about it."

Whoa. I looked at her hands. Her right hand, gripping the spoon, trembled a little, but her left hand wasn't moving the way I'd expected. Then I looked at her face. Still Meredith. That was a big step for Mom, to say she didn't want to do something without Gatekeeper sending somebody else out to help. I wondered if Dad saw it. She really was getting stronger.

She raised her chin, and the light caught the long scar on her throat. A thin, faint, horizontal line.

I looked away.

After dinner, I went upstairs to do email and start my homework.

Nothing from Jeff, so I just wrote him a short note. I'd found two great new words but figured I'd better hit him with just one at a time, so I left out the little Hawaiian fish. After all, it's hard to keep your email short with a word like humuhumunukunukuapuaa.

To: jeffers@moondog.com
From: bankrobber@cvc.org
Subject:

Hey Jefferson. Saw my shrink again today and he had a terrific black eye. One of his clients punched him. Maybe I should reconsider my career path.☺

Hey, new word. Pecos. It means to shoot a man and roll his body into the river. Not sure how I'll ever use that one.

Later $

As the message disappeared into cyberspace, I leaned back and considered. It had been a while since I'd written more than a sentence or two to Jeff. I didn't feel too bad about that, since lately I was lucky to get even that much from him. What tennis had done to my free time, Rose was doing to his. But I didn't want to let it go too far. Was Jeff ever going to get a phone?

For the first time, I wondered how he communicated with Rose. Maybe they just spent all their time together. No need for a phone that way.

Leaning forward, I started typing again.

To: jeffers@moondog.com
From: bankrobber@cvc.org
Subject:

Hey Jefferson I really wish you were here to talk to. Sometimes it's like everything's changing and I can't keep up with it. Yesterday when I was driving home from tennis, I realized I'm already better friends with those guys than I ever was with Rob and Kevin. Okay, this sounds stupid, but I always used to laugh when they said something that was supposed to be funny even though I didn't think it was. Like when they'd talk about me raping and pillaging because I'm a Viking. Not funny, but I'd laugh. I never do that with the tennis guys. I thought it was such a bad thing Rob cutting me out like that. But it's like it opened things up to be more me.

Okay, that sounds really really stupid. If I actually send this instead of deleting it you'll know I definitely need a shrink.

I think what scares me the most is I get mad sometimes now. You always poked at me about how I never got mad ever no matter what happened. Well that's changing and it scares me. But this tennis thing is probably the scariest of all because it's so great and what if it goes away.

Cripes. I'm all over the place.

I'm reaching for the send key.

I'm actually going to send this trash.

It's going going ahhhhhhh

Gone! I leaned back and blew out my breath. This was by far my weirdest email ever. I should have just deleted it.

On the other hand, it would be interesting to see what Jeff had to say.

As long as he didn't go back to ☹ again.

Thursday morning, I pulled my Spanish book out of my locker, fumbled, and dropped it. The book hit my toe and skidded toward Tara's locker.

She was intent on working her combination. As I stepped forward and bent to pick up my book, I watched her fingers twirl the dial. Smooth and easy. Either she'd tried the WD-40 trick, or she'd ignored Alex and brought a different lock.

That last option wouldn't surprise me. The supermodel had a sassy swing to her attitudes as well as her walk.

Sassy. Good word. Short but expressive.

Her fingers were long and slender. Pretty. They stopped spinning the dial and tightened on the lock but didn't jerk it open. Puzzled, I glanced from her hands to her face. She was watching me, shoulders hunched, eyes scared. *Uh-oh.*

This made the third time Tara had caught me staring.

I straightened up and gave her a sorry-about-that smile, but it didn't seem to help. Maybe I should say something about her lock working better now. But then she'd get the idea I stared at her all the time, and that definitely wouldn't help.

Shrugging, I turned back to my locker. For a guy who liked words, I wasn't all that great at using them. Better just let it go.

"Hey, Tara."

Hearing her name, I looked over again in spite of myself.

114

Alex had come up behind her, facing me so she stood between us.

He wasn't a big guy, but somehow he seemed to loom over and around Tara as he leaned his hand against the next locker, partly blocking her in. Just like he'd done that first day. That time, her reaction had reminded me of my mom, but just for a second. Then the supermodel had come back out and handled things.

Today, though, Tara was off-balance. Because of me. I saw the panic, saw that somebody little and scared was out. She was going to run.

Without thinking, I started toward her.

Fear always turned my mom silent. But Tara sounded like a train whistle on steroids as she ducked under Alex's arm and took off down the hall. I would've gone after her, the way I always did with Mom, but the wave of echoing sound pushed me back. It was horrible. High, terrified, loud enough to knock holes in your eardrums.

Alex spun to watch her go. As the sound cut off, he turned sharply back, looking as shocked as I felt. "What did you *do* to her?" he demanded into the sudden silence.

Everybody had been staring after Tara. Now their attention switched to Alex and me. From a few yards away, Rob watched me without expression. He had one arm around Mandy and the other hand on Lovejoy's shoulder, as if I might lunge across the hall to attack them next.

Lovejoy. After one glance, I kept my face turned away.

"I didn't do anything." My voice sounded flat. Lame. Unconvincing.

"Yeah, sure." Alex moved closer. "That's why she's scared to death of you. What did you do to her that night in the parking lot?"

The cooked noodle swelled and stretched until everyone in the universe could see me. I looked away from Alex and focused on my open locker. With slow, careful movements, I stepped toward it. I shut and locked the door, then gave the dial the usual half turn to make sure it was really locked. Locked up good and tight.

"Bank." Alex's voice came from a mile or so below me.

Staring straight ahead, high above the upturned faces all around me, I walked toward the stairs and my first-hour Spanish class. Behind me, the silence cracked apart into whispers, mutters, and bubbles of excited talk.

It sounded a lot like humuhumunukunukuapuaa.

My name, swimming like a little Hawaiian fish from person to person down the endless hallway.

20

Walls

Our false spring broke that night.

Lying in bed, I heard the wind swell out of the north, rattling my windows and moaning under the eaves. Papers on my desk stirred as cold air sneaked through invisible openings around the closed windows. One rustled its way to the edge of the desk and sailed to the floor.

The first splatters of rain hit the glass. *Plunk. Plunk. Plunk-plunk.*

I should get up and shut the outside storm windows before the rain really got going. And while I was up, I should get socks and the sweats I'd abandoned during these warm nights, or I'd be freezing by morning. I should also set my phone alarm, in case this turned into a thunderstorm and knocked out the electricity.

I didn't do any of those things. I stayed in bed, staring at the dark ceiling. I wished it *would* storm, with cataclysmic violence, and blow our whole house away. With me inside. That would give me a good excuse not to go to school tomorrow.

Turning on my side, I pulled the comforter up to my ears.

Today could have been a lot worse. I wasn't important enough for rumors to shoot through school the way they would for somebody who already had a reputation. With all the confusion about what had really happened this morning, most people didn't seem to know I'd even been involved.

In second-hour computer lab, some girls behind me were saying Tara had gotten bad news from home. One girl knew for sure somebody in her family had died. "Her older brother," she said in a hushed voice. "I think it was a car wreck."

As the day went on, I heard several variations on that rumor. My name did come up a few times, though I never caught what people were saying about me. Once I walked by just as a guy said, "What happened with Alex White and that new girl? She's kind of weird, isn't she?"

That bothered me more than anything. I wanted to protect Tara, to rescue her. Instead, I'd made things worse for her.

The same way I did for Lovejoy.

Clutching the comforter, I groaned and rolled over to face the wall. The rain pounded down hard now, beating steadily on the roof.

What was *wrong* with me? Here I was, a sophomore in high school, but like some bratty third-grader, I couldn't even get close to a girl without knocking her down or making her run away screaming.

Even Trish Vespers, who was probably the nicest person I knew. The other day, she'd asked if I'd heard anything from Jeff. Like an idiot, I told her all about Rose. I went on and on about how he was so crazy about this girl he couldn't think or talk about anything else. It wasn't until I walked off that it hit me why Trish kept saying, "Wow, that's great. I'm happy for him," and sounding so fake.

I knew Trish had a major crush on Jeff. How could I have forgotten?

You'd think with all these years of watching out for my mom, I'd be better with girls. More sensitive. Instead, it looked like Dad was right.

My life was weirder than I realized.

And so was I.

Lightning didn't strike our house that night, and we didn't blow away or get squashed by falling trees. In the morning, my alarm went off as usual. I shivered my way out of bed and into a hot shower.

"What's wrong, Bank?" Mom asked when I went into the kitchen.

"Nothing," I mumbled.

She didn't push it. "You remember your dad left early this morning on a business trip? He'll be gone a few days."

"Oh, right." At least that was good news. I definitely didn't want questions from Dad, and it seemed he always gave me the most attention when I least wanted it.

A cold wind slammed waves of rain against the Prizm's windshield as if determined to smash it. Not tennis weather. When I got to school, I stood inside the front door, dripping, and checked my book bag to see if I could avoid going to my locker.

No luck. On Fridays, we always did a section in our Spanish workbook, and I didn't have mine with me. I headed upstairs, feeling like a giraffe that had to get to the water hole even though it knew dozens of lions crouched in wait.

I edged around the corner and sneaked a look at Tara's locker. She wasn't there. Lovejoy was, though. Before I could duck out of sight, she saw me and crutched energetically forward. I braced myself.

"Bank." She sounded breathless. "What're you doing for lunch?"

"Um, eating."

She laughed. "I want to talk to you. But you're always at the fuzzhead table."

119

Lovejoy wanted to talk to me?

"Sometimes I go up to the computer lab," I said. "I bring my lunch."

"Well, can I meet you there? Today?"

Lovejoy wanted to talk to me. Was this a good thing? She was friends with Tara. I might not like hearing what she had to say.

"Bank?" She leaned forward and knocked on my chest. "Are you in there?"

I nodded.

"I didn't pack a lunch today," she said. "So I'll have to buy something and bring it up to the lab. Is that okay?"

"Um, sure."

"Good. See you then." She wheeled, bright-colored ribbons swaying as she swung away. She'd gotten pretty good with those crutches.

Yesterday, after Tara's meltdown, I'd avoided Max and Rajid so they wouldn't have a chance to avoid me. I went into math class at the last minute and sat on the other side of the room. Instead of joining them at lunch, I sneaked back up to my computer lab hidey-hole.

It was miserable. Lonely.

Now, at the thought of Lovejoy there with me, my heart did a sort of jump-and-roll. A second later, it somersaulted even higher as somebody whacked me on the back.

"Hey, man! Where'd you go yesterday? I thought we were getting some tennis after school."

Max, with Rajid standing patiently behind him.

"Sorry, I…something came up." Lame.

"You didn't sit with us at lunch, either." Max's face, as open as a little kid's, looked puzzled and reproachful. "Something wrong?"

I took a deep breath. "Didn't you hear about yesterday morning? That thing with Tara Prentiss?"

"I heard she was screeching in the halls. What happened?"

"It's kind of hard to explain." Try *impossible*. "I can't without telling something I don't, well, don't have the right to tell. But it was sort of my fault. I figured everybody in school hated me." I shrugged. "Guess I didn't want to be around people."

"Why?" Max sounded as if somebody had offered me a million dollars and I'd turned it down. "You should've told us, man. We'll stick with you."

Rajid spoke up. "If you cut off Max's arms and legs and left him out in the desert, he'd roll along the sand until he found somebody so he wouldn't die alone. Max *never* doesn't want to be around people. Not like me."

I grinned, relieved. "Me neither."

Max looked from Rajid to me. "You guys are *strange*."

By the time I walked into first-hour Spanish, I felt a little better about myself. But whenever I thought about Tara, I felt sick. When Mom had tried to kill herself that time, it had been my fault. What if Tara—

A deep growl interrupted my thoughts. "Buenos días, clase."

Señora Gott stood in front of the class, face grim, body language threatening. We mumbled reluctant hellos back at her. Our Spanish teacher was actually German, and I'd decided early on that she must be a descendant of Adolf Hitler. Maybe I should switch to Latin.

She ordered us to get our workbooks out and put on the headphones. First she said this in Spanish, then in English when most kids looked blank, even though it was the same thing she said every Friday. As I dug out my book and got set up, bits and pieces of things I knew about DID rolled through my head.

Something really bad must have happened to Tara. Probably when she was little. Had her parents done it?

Out of the corner of my eye, I saw Señora Gott pounce on a kid who was goofing off and didn't see her coming. I bent over and clamped on the headphones. The language lab hadn't been designed for somebody my height, and the headphone wires didn't reach far enough for me to sit up straight. I stared down at my open workbook.

Dr. Sam had told Mom that somebody important, deep inside, still didn't know about the bad things her foster parents had done to her. She would have to deal with that if she wanted to get well. But she had to move carefully. Most of the alters didn't know the ugly years had been over for a long time. They didn't believe she was safe. They would violently oppose taking down the protective walls and letting the memories come together.

"Sometimes," Mom had said, looking down and speaking so quietly I could hardly hear, "I'm afraid it will be too much."

Sometimes I was scared of that, too. And now Tara—

I jumped as a heavy hand clamped onto my shoulder. A blood-red fingernail stabbed at my blank workbook.

I peered up at Señora Gott's scowling face. "Lo siento mucho, Señora Gott." *Sorry, ma'am.*

She glared. "You're not even on the right page, Señor Grande."

She'd just called me Mister Big. How about that for rude? Picking up the headphones, which had jerked off when she startled me into straightening up, I rubbed my ears.

Whew. How did Tara do it? High school was hard enough without something like DID.

122

21

Pecos

Since Lovejoy had to buy her lunch, it wasn't surprising the computer lab was empty when I got there. Not surprising, but disappointing.

Surprisingly disappointing.

I ate one of my peanut butter sandwiches while I waited, as a sort of appetizer. I also checked my email. I'd been too down to do that yesterday, so two days' worth had built up. For me, that still wasn't much, and almost all of it was junk. But I'd finally gotten a good letter from Jeff.

> To: bankrobber@cvc.org
> From: jeffers@moondog.com
> Subject:
>
> Bro, you can do a lot better than Rob and Kev. Rob used to be okay, but now he's all about himself. Kev's just Kev. At our 75th high school reunion he won't look or sound any different, and he won't have a clue why nobody else is there (we'll all be dead of old age).
>
> Here's the good news. Sam got a part-time job and they hired me too. I can ride with him until I get my license in May. That means $ and that means phone! I have my eye on this really cool one that

just came out, but I'll probably have to go cheaper. You're right. I've been spending most of my allowance on Rose and she said I need to cool it. She wrote out a list of cheap/free dates. She's amazing.

And here's the best news

As the doorknob rattled, I looked up. The heat of anticipation fired up inside my head and shot all the way to my toenails. The door swung wide.

In buzzed The Bee, with a CD case in her hand.

She stopped, looking even more startled than I felt. At least I'd been expecting somebody.

"Um, hello, Mrs. Benderbee."

She stared in turn at the peanut butter sandwich in my hand, the Dr Pepper sitting next to the keyboard, and the email open on the computer monitor.

"You are…" She paused. It took me a second to realize she expected me to finish the sentence.

"Bank Jonsson." I sat up straight and set my sandwich carefully on its baggie. I could hear Dad's voice in my head. *Bank, stand up. You're being rude.* I pushed to my feet. "I'm in Mr. Laptop—I mean, Mr. Lattup's computer class."

"I know who you are, Bank." She walked to his desk and set the CD case down. "But why are you here now?"

Obviously, she didn't intend to just shrug and walk off. She wasn't being ugly about it, but I could tell she didn't like the combination of no scheduled class, no Mr. Laptop, and me at the computer with food and drink.

Then Lovejoy swung into the doorway.

I was directly in her line of sight. The Bee wasn't.

"Hey, Bank," Lovejoy said. "Sorry it took me so long." She crutched in, ribbons flying, curly hair bouncing, brown eyes sparkling with fun.

The Bee's eyebrows must've shot up a full inch. "Lovejoy Fox. What are *you* doing here?"

Lovejoy's mouth opened. I could see the options scrolling down behind her eyes and landing on the rejection pile, one after another. Nothing she could say would sound acceptable to a high school principal.

"Lunch," she said and blushed deeply.

So. I'd finally found a use for my great new word. Pecos. Just shoot me and roll my body into the river.

Right now, please.

"All right, Bank and Lovejoy." The Bee shut her office door behind us. "Have a seat and tell me what's going on. How long have you two been meeting up there?"

She sat behind her desk and leaned back, crossing her arms. She looked authoritative and ready to challenge any attempts to worm out of trouble. When you're a high school principal who never quite made it to five feet tall, body language is everything.

I suspected she had a pillow on the seat of her chair, too. A thick one.

Lovejoy sighed. "We—"

"Mrs. Benderbee," I said. "I know about Tara Prentiss."

Her expression sharpened. "And just what is it you know about her?"

"I know she has DID. Dissociative Identity Disorder."

It would've been more accurate to say I was pretty sure she had DID, but this situation called for confidence. It paid off, too. The Bee didn't deny anything, and she uncrossed her arms and leaned

125

forward. "I assume there's a reason you're telling me this."

I nodded. "Did you hear about what happened yesterday morning? At Tara's locker?"

"Yes, I did. I called her parents to come and take her home. I couldn't get many details, but I understand something frightened her." She waved a hand. "Go ahead and eat, Lovejoy. I don't want you fainting on us this afternoon."

"It was mostly me," I said. "I scared her, I mean. But not on purpose."

While I explained what had happened, Lovejoy held her hamburger in one hand but didn't bite into it. I glanced over when a blob of mustard dropped onto her jeans. She was listening, brown eyes fixed on my face, lips slightly parted. She hadn't even noticed the mustard.

When I finished, The Bee nodded. "Thank you, Bank. You've explained it very well. But how do you happen to know about…"

Her eyes flicked to her watch. She frowned, and her body language tightened up again. "I don't see what this has to do with the two of you meeting up in the computer lab."

I spoke fast, before Lovejoy could say anything. "I wanted to talk to her with nobody else around. I was going to ask her to talk to Tara. You know, explain what happened. Tell her I'm safe. If she trusts Lovejoy, Tara might even be okay about coming with her to meet me. I want her to know she can trust me, and why."

The Bee's face told me she wanted to know why, too. But she just said, "From what I know of both of you, I'm willing to accept your explanation. But I'd suggest you stay out of the classrooms at lunchtime. I'll be checking on that room from time to time." She turned to Lovejoy. "Do you have anything to add?"

Lovejoy shook her head.

"Well, finish your lunch quickly, both of you. You'll be late to class, but I'll send excuse slips with you." She pulled a pad of pink forms out of the top drawer.

126

I was expert at getting food down fast, but lunch gave Lovejoy a bad case of hiccups. As we went through the empty halls, I could hear a little *huck* every few seconds, along with the rhythmic thump of her rubber-tipped crutches and the swish as she swung herself forward for each step.

"How much longer do you have to use those?" I asked.

"What?"

"The crutches."

"Oh."

Obviously, her thoughts were somewhere else. I sighed. Once again, contact with me hadn't exactly improved Lovejoy's life.

"I have a doctor appointment Tuesday. I should know then." She shook her head. "Bank, why did you say you'd asked me to meet you? I—" She closed her lips tightly on a hiccup. "I didn't expect you to lie."

"I didn't. I said I wanted to talk to you about Tara, and that's true. I've seen you with her, so I figured you're friends."

"But you made it sound like *you* were the one who asked to get together."

"Yeah, but I didn't actually say that." Her persistence surprised me. Most kids seemed to lie more easily than they told the truth, much less care about what anyone else said. "I couldn't just let you take the blame."

"But I *was* to blame." She stopped. "This is my class. I'll see you later, Bank."

"Okay. Sure." I turned away. When I didn't hear her crutches start up again, I looked back. She was watching me. As I saw her expression, my heart did a jump-and-roll the way it had earlier today. My voice sounded hoarse as I said, "Lovejoy."

"What?"

"Why did you want to talk to me?"

She smiled. "I have to go in. Mr. Anders already saw me."

"Do you—would you like to—"

"Sure." The smile curled, and her eyes sparkled. "I have to

talk to Mr. Grover for a couple of minutes after school. Meet me at my locker, okay?"

I nodded.

She swung herself through the doorway. I headed for fourth-hour English, grinning like an idiot. Maybe we'd finally broken the curse.

This felt *way* better than tennis. This time, "chuffed" didn't even begin to cover it.

22

Hyenas

When I went into class and handed Ms. Montoya my pink excuse, everybody stared.

That happened every time someone walked in late, though, so I didn't think anything about it. I went over and sat by Rajid. He barely glanced at me. But since kids were looking our way, and I knew he was a reserved kind of guy, I didn't think much about that, either.

"All right, people," Ms. Montoya drawled. "I realize this class is so incredibly boring, it's high excitement to watch Bank come in and sit down."

Kids laughed. My face heated up.

She patted the book on her desk. "But now let's get back to *Lord of the Flies*. We were discussing symbolism in the hunt scene. Page one thirty-three."

If Señora Gott sounded like she should be teaching German instead of Spanish, Ms. Montoya looked as if she should take on my Spanish class instead of English. Her accent was pure Oklahoma, though. Everybody liked her, and I thought she was a good teacher. If anybody could get us through that revolting scene with the pig, Ms. Montoya could. I pulled out my book, opened it, and paid attention.

After class, I squeezed out from behind my desk. Picking up my book bag, I turned to Rajid. "You and Max playing after school today?"

He shook his head.

"Oh. Well, I can't today anyway. I *think* I've got a date." I grinned, expecting a reaction, but his face stayed serious.

"That's good." He hoisted his book bag onto one shoulder.

We walked out together. "Well, see you next week," I said.

He nodded and walked off. I'd hoped he might say something about this weekend. Where did the guys on the team practice when they couldn't play outside? Trevor had told me a coach had to stay if anyone wanted to use the courtroom after school hours, so that usually didn't work on weekends.

Too bad we didn't play tennis in P.E. I trotted down the stairs toward the gym. We just dinked around with time-wasters like badminton, volleyball, and contorting ourselves into bizarre shapes on the parallel bars.

With at least two months of ugly weather ahead of us, I sure didn't want to wait that long to play tennis again. I'd have to ask Trevor.

For no obvious reason, my mind hopped to Lovejoy. I was grinning when I walked into the locker room.

"Jonsson!" A voice cut through the usual clatter of guys insulting each other and banging locker doors. "What're you so happy about? Got something going tonight?"

The noisy room went quieter than I'd ever heard it. The only sound came from a dripping shower.

I tracked the voice to a big, round-headed guy at a locker halfway across the room. Everybody called him Bingo. I knew him by reputation as a deadhead, part of the drink-and-drive group. And I knew him by locker room experience as one of those guys whose jokes and comments about girls left you feeling like you'd been chewing on a used gym sock. Or worse.

"Um," I said. Not the most brilliant comeback.

"Gym parking lot, huh? Stupid." Even before his words sank all the way in, I knew I didn't like either the look on Bingo's face or the way everyone else was listening. "There's better places for that, you know."

My face prickled, and I took a deep breath. "I don't know what you're talking about."

What a cliché. Besides, it must've been obvious to everybody that I knew exactly what he was talking about. Tara. I heard Alex's voice. *What did you do to her that night in the parking lot?* I stumbled as I turned toward my gym locker.

Bingo laughed. "If you need help, just let me know." He gave me a thumbs up, followed by a cruder gesture, and pulled his shirt off over his head.

So. Word had spread.

Turning my back on the room, I dragged my gym clothes out of the locker. A guy dropped his phone onto the wet tiles and let out a splutter of profanity. Somebody laughed, a couple of guys pushed in through the door, and the noise bumped up to its usual level.

I tried to shrug it off. Crisis over. Bingo was always poking at somebody, and today it just happened to be me.

Our class had moved on to volleyball, which should've been great for me because of my height. Two problems with that. I didn't like volleyball, and I wasn't any good at it.

With tennis, I didn't even think about how I looked when I ran. No cooked noodle or hunted giraffe images. But volleyball was torture. My arms flailed, my hands hit everything except the ball, and my legs tripped me and anyone who got too close. Coach Summers had finally told me to stay on the back row instead of rotating with everyone else. That way, at least I had fewer people around to get tangled up with.

Gloomily, I shuffled out of the locker room and lined up on the back row. *Let the Games begin.*

The first time the ball hit my head, I thought it was an accident. Maybe it was. Maybe that just gave them the idea. But whether it started on purpose or not, by the fourth or fifth time, there was no question. Kids were actually aiming at me. Not the other team—guys on my own side. I looked around for Coach, but he'd turned away to argue with a kid holding out a pink excuse.

131

No help there.

This must be what a giraffe felt like when lions ambushed and pulled it down. No, not lions. More like hyenas. Something mean and cowardly that swarmed around just out of reach. Darting in to bite and tear, then slinking away before the giraffe could get in a good kick.

At first, I tried keeping my hands up to protect myself. Besides looking stupid, that didn't do any good. One time the ball just smashed my finger into my own mouth.

I couldn't fight back, couldn't protect myself, and couldn't run away. If I ran now, I'd be a pathetic loser the rest of my life. All I could do was wait it out and hope Coach noticed before things got too bad.

So much for hope. Coach turned back to us as the ball bounced off my ear, but he just frowned. He hadn't seen enough to get the idea.

The end came when the guy serving for our side, a strong player named Josh Sanderson, sacrificed a possible point for the satisfaction of slamming the ball into my face from two feet away. The impact knocked me down. I was sure it had either squashed my eye flat or popped it out of the socket.

"What's *wrong* with you guys?" Finally, Coach came storming in, shoving Josh away. "You trying to kill him?"

He crouched beside me and tried to pull my hand off my right eye. No way. The pressure of that hand was the only thing holding me together.

"Come on, Bank. Just for a second, buddy. Then you can put it back."

I couldn't see, since my left eye had clamped shut in sympathy, but I heard his voice change direction as he turned away from me. "Back off. I can't see a thing with you jokers hanging over us. Sanderson, pushups for you. One hundred. Flinders, count for him."

I felt my fingers peeled carefully up. A pause, then the

comforting pressure was back. Coach turned away again, and I heard the word "hospital."

I was home by dinnertime, but for once I didn't feel like eating. I'd thrown up a couple of times on the way to the hospital, but the painkillers took care of that. Now I was mostly just sleepy. They'd given me something a lot stronger than aspirin.

Poor old Viking Clone. I should've been nicer to him on Wednesday.

The specialist they'd called to the emergency room had done a lot of tests. Then he sat back, smiled, and assured me I wouldn't lose my eye or any part of my sight. He said the strong, prominent bones around my eye had taken most of the impact and protected it from real injury. I wouldn't feel or look so great for a while, but by Monday I should be okay to go to school.

Wonderful. Just what I wanted to do. Go back among the hyenas.

No concussion either, but Mom insisted on having me downstairs where she could keep an eye on me. She made up the sofa with blankets and pillows, turned off all but one dim light, and tucked me in. Nice.

"Hope?" I mumbled. Hope was the alter with a soft spot for anybody who was sick or in pain.

"No. Hope went in for good, remember?" I felt the weight of another cover settle over me. Warm fingers pulled it up under my chin. "She's part of me now."

"Part of Me?" Confusing…

"Part of me, your mom. Not Me, the name."

"Oh."

From there, I must've slid straight down into sleep. Next thing I knew, people were talking not far away, using quiet voices. Who? Where was I? My eyes didn't want to open, and I didn't care enough to put much effort into it. I wished they'd go away so I could sleep. Hoping they'd take the hint, I yawned hugely. *Ouch.* I grunted with pain and fumbled a hand toward my face. My fingers got caught under the covers, and I gave up.

"I'm sorry. I didn't mean to wake you." Soft words, closer now. Cool and sweet. Not Mom's.

"Piggy," I muttered.

"What did you say?" Bubbles of laughter rose in the words. I felt them pop lightly on my forehead as reality blurred and fell apart. I disappeared into sleep.

I'd been dreaming. *Lord of the Flies*, and I was Piggy. I'd read ahead in the book, and I knew what was coming for him.

He didn't deserve it either.

23

Accuse

"What we really need," Lovejoy said, "is to talk to Tara."

Lovejoy had come over to spend Sunday afternoon with me. After two days of sleeping and eating, I felt a lot better. My right eye still wouldn't open all the way, but it didn't hurt as much as I'd expected. The swelling wasn't as bad, either. The skin around my eye had gone all crazy colors and looked ridiculous, though, so I tried to keep my left side toward Lovejoy.

As for what was going on with the inside of my head, that was a mix, too. Lovejoy, her bad ankle propped on our coffee table and her curly head resting against the back of our sofa, counted as a major positive. The printed-out email in her hand didn't.

I picked up my drink. "Talking to Tara wouldn't help. Probably just make things worse."

"Why?"

"Come on. Let's take a break." I reached for her glass. "Another Dr Pepper?"

"Could I have water instead?"

"Nope, sorry. We don't have water."

She looked up quickly, lips parted. As her mouth curled into a smile and her eyes sparkled, I realized I was getting addicted to seeing that happen. The best was when *I* made it happen, like now.

"You dork." She punched my arm. "For a tenth of a second, I actually believed you."

"Half a second," I said. "I counted."

The kitchen door was shut. I grinned. Mom must be giving us

privacy. She never closed this door, which explained the creaky hinges when I pulled it open. My dad, the king of WD-40, had missed this one.

As I walked in, I heard Mom coughing. The room looked smoky and smelled like a minor forest fire. She was sliding a tray into the oven with one hand, waving smoke away with the other.

"The cookies aren't ready yet, Bank," she said. "The first batch burned."

I set our glasses on the counter and shoved up the window over the sink. Then I opened the back door, pulling in a blast of cold air. The smoke swirled and thinned right away.

"What happened?" I'd never known her to burn anything when she cooked.

"Fighter came out, and she wouldn't go back in." Mom's eyes looked teary, but that might've just been the smoke. "She's angry about Dr. Sam and how things are changing. She keeps pushing her way out. I think she let the cookies burn on purpose."

"The smoke alarm didn't go off." I looked at the ceiling. "Hey, it's gone."

"I know. I put it in the refrigerator."

"Why?"

"I always do when I cook. It's so sensitive, Bank. It goes off any time I use the oven, and it makes such an awful noise."

I wouldn't know. All I ever did was heat things up in the microwave.

"I'm sorry," she whispered. "I shouldn't have done that. It wasn't safe, was it?"

"Hey, it's okay, Mom." I put my arms around her, and she leaned against me. Did this count as being overprotective? Dad kept telling me to back off, but this had really upset her. "It's fine. Shutting it in the fridge was a good idea."

After a few seconds, she asked, "Bank, are you crying?"

"No. I'm laughing. I'm sorry." I'd been trying not to, but— "That's pretty creative, Mom. Putting the smoke alarm in the fridge,

136

I mean. I wouldn't have thought of that."

She pushed me away, but I was relieved to see her smiling.

"You need to get back to your friend." She picked up the potholder. "And I want to make sure this batch doesn't burn, too."

"You should get Fighter to integrate. Get her out of the way for good. Maybe you could swap her for Libby."

She looked up at me, dark eyes reproachful.

"Sorry," I said. "Just a joke." A bad one.

She waved the potholder at a stray wisp of smoke. "I did think integration would go faster, after those first five went in. It's almost as if the rest are...I don't know, waiting for something. A signal. An event. Something." She sighed. "Dr. Sam said it doesn't help to hurry things. She says I'm doing fine. But Fighter *is* getting pushier."

I wouldn't put it past Fighter to make Mom burn all the cookies. "Ask Gatekeeper not to let her out till you're done."

"Oh, he tried. He doesn't have much control over her anymore."

That was a little scary. "Why not?"

She leaned close and whispered, "Actually, he just pretends he doesn't. She likes to think she's too tough for him." Her eyelids flickered, and she muttered, "I heard that."

"Back off, okay, Fighter? I'm talking to Meredith." It wasn't easy to tell secrets around the different alters. "When does Dad get home?"

"Sometime Thursday. He's driving, so there's no set schedule."

The timer on the stove buzzed, and she turned away. I poured Dr Pepper into both glasses and left her peering into the oven.

Lovejoy hesitated before she took her glass. "Thanks. Is everything okay? I smell smoke."

"Mom burned some cookies." I sat beside her. "She's embarrassed about it, so don't say anything when she comes in. Okay?"

137

"My mom *never* burns cookies." She took a sip and licked the rim of her glass. "She buys them at Quik-Mart."

"What does your dad think about that?" Store-bought definitely wouldn't be okay with mine. He loved all the homemade stuff. Mom even baked our bread, and Dad and I could eat a loaf apiece when they first came out of the oven.

"I don't have a dad. They divorced before I was born. I think he lives in North Dakota now."

"Oh. Wow, I'm sorry."

"It's okay. I'm used to it. I wouldn't know him if I saw him." Her smile didn't look as curly as usual. "If you still have your original parents, Bank, you're one in a thousand. And if they still like each other, you're one in a million." She leaned forward and set her drink on the table. "And since your mom actually bakes cookies, you're more like one in about *ten* million."

Here I'd thought we were different because of DID. I hadn't realized it was all about keeping our smoke alarm in the fridge.

"Besides," she said, "your family has the best water I've ever tasted."

"What?"

She pointed to her glass.

"That's not—" I remembered. "You wanted *water*. I'm sorry. I'll—"

I reached for her glass, but she caught my hand. "It's okay. I shouldn't have said anything."

When I leaned back again, she kept hold of my hand. That should've been awkward, but it played out like tennis—somehow my hand knew what to do, turning under hers so our fingers could lock. Hers felt small and surprisingly rough. As my pulse rate shot up, the tender skin around my eye stung. I turned my head toward her, but she was looking down. All I could see was the top of her head.

Sometimes being tall has disadvantages. I liked her curls, but they didn't tell me much. I wanted to see her eyes.

I heard the creaky hinges of the kitchen door. "Hey," I said. "Cookies."

What a romantic guy.

Lovejoy smiled up at me, then squeezed my hand and pulled her fingers away. "Terrific. I'm starving."

Mom didn't hang around after she said hello and set the plate on the coffee table, but I could tell she was okay with Lovejoy. Four or five alters popped out for a few seconds, too, and nobody acted worried. Fighter stayed in, which was probably a good thing.

"She likes you," I said, once we were alone again.

"I like her, too. We had a great talk Friday night." Lovejoy picked up a cookie and examined it. "Wow, chocolate chip. And they're warm." She took a bite and closed her eyes. "Mmmm."

"Friday night?" Volleyball, hospital, painkillers, crashing on the sofa, crazy dreams. "When did you talk to Mom?"

Eyes still shut, she held up a hand. "This is too good, Bank. Just let me eat in peace, okay?"

I snagged a couple of cookies and munched them down.

Friday night. I'd almost forgotten about the voice, the bubbles of laughter, and the touch on my forehead. They'd blurred into my dreams. If I'd thought about it, I would have figured some alter I didn't recognize had come out then. Maybe somebody taking over Hope's job.

But maybe not.

"Did you come to our house Friday night?" I asked.

"We *were* supposed to get together after school, you know." She opened her eyes. "I came over to see how you were doing. Then I was sorry I woke you. You looked pretty bad."

I hoped she meant the black eye, and not that I was drooling onto my pillow or something. "Wow, thanks. For coming, I mean."

"No problem." She studied the cookies and chose two. I noticed she picked the biggest ones. "This is going to take more self-control than I have, Bank. Would you please hide the rest of these?"

While she held a hand over her eyes and sang the North High

139

fight song, I snagged a handful of cookies for myself and carried the plate away. Sliding it under a magazine by Dad's chair. I grinned. Lovejoy Fox had to be the most fun person I'd ever met. Her singing voice was terrible, but that obviously didn't bother her.

I heard the kitchen door open. Mom probably wondered what in the world was going on. We weren't used to so much liveliness around here.

"Okay," I said as I sat down again. Then, louder, "All clear."

"Go! Win!" Dropping the hand she'd been punching into the air, she took the other off her eyes and reached for one of her cookies. "Thanks. Wow, is that clock right? Mom's picking me up in half an hour. And we still need to talk about this."

"About what?"

"This." Holding up the piece of paper, she waved it at me.

I groaned. I didn't *want* to talk about it, but she was right. We had to. That paper was the reason the hyenas had tried to knock my head off with a volleyball.

The disaster at Tara's locker had happened on Thursday. Friday morning, somebody sent an email to almost everyone at school. They used an address nobody had ever heard of, which probably meant the person had created a new one just for this. A lot of kids wouldn't have seen the email until after school, except that somebody printed it out just before lunch and ran off copies—who or why, nobody knew—and scattered them around the cafeteria tables. Then the word really spread.

I must've been the last person at North to know about the email. I hadn't heard until today, when Lovejoy pulled a copy out of her purse and showed me.

"Okay. Let me read it again." I reached for the paper, took a deep breath, and started from the top.

Bank Jonsson attacked Tara Prentiss.

According to this, Tara had gone outside during halftime of the basketball game, saying the gym was too hot and noisy. I watched her go, followed her, and enticed her to the dark end of the

140

parking lot. Then I jumped her. She fought me off and ran back to her friends. She was in shock, so she didn't tell anyone what had happened.

I read through the email twice. Just a made-up story, somebody else's word against mine. Nobody who knew me would believe it.

But who at school really knew me? Not Rob and Kevin, not anymore. Jeff had moved hundreds of miles away.

And whoever wrote this gave details that sounded convincing even to me. They said Tara had been afraid of me from her first day at North because of the creepy way I looked at her. She asked some girls who I was and told them I kept staring at her. A guy I used to hang out with said he'd noticed that, too. He'd stopped hanging out with me because he didn't like the way I looked at girls and joked about things like rape. The night of the game, he'd wondered why I never came back after I went outside at halftime. He also said I'd knocked another girl down and pretended it was an accident.

The letter ended, *Tara didn't want to tell and she won't go to the police. But if everybody knows what kind of creep Bank Jonsson is, that might keep it from happening to somebody else.*

No wonder everybody hated me.

I touched the puffy skin under my eye. When those guys were pelting me with the volleyball, an ugly excitement had vibrated in the air. Guys my own age, some I'd known since kindergarten. They *wanted* to hurt me. Maybe even kill me.

Lord of the Flies. Piggy and Simon. Or maybe I was more like Ralph. Ralph and I might have nightmares, but at least we'd survived.

I turned and saw Lovejoy watching me. All the fun had died out of her face. Her gaze dropped to the paper in my hands.

"It's true, isn't it?" she said.

24

Untangling

"You think it's *true*?"

I couldn't believe it. Spending the afternoon with me must have convinced Lovejoy I really was the conhead the email claimed. Earlier, when she took my hand, was that just a test to see if I would grab at her? But I didn't grab *at* her. I just held her hand, like a normal person. She'd been the one to pull away, sure, but only because Mom came in with cookies.

"I know it's true." She plucked the paper out of my fingers. "Exactly the way this bit about me is. You did knock me down, and you did say it was an accident. Because it was."

Now I was even more confused. "Do you think I did it, or don't you?"

"Tara's beautiful. I don't blame you for gawking at her."

Gawking. Another good word, but I didn't like having it applied to me. It sounded as if I went around with my eyes bugged out and my mouth sagging open.

"Everybody gawks at Tara," I said. "You should've seen them at that basketball game when she walked into the gym. If I hadn't gawked, I would've been the only person there who didn't."

"I know. That's why I don't like hanging out with her. It makes me feel invisible."

A thin edge of hope slid through my confusion. "So what do you think I actually did?"

"Stared at Tara. Probably more than you knew, and definitely more than you knew *she* knew."

I worked my way through that last sentence. "So, you mean even when she acted like she didn't notice I was looking at her, she did?"

What *I* noticed now was that Lovejoy's cheeks and the tip of her nose had gone pink, and she didn't quite meet my eyes. Before I could figure out what that meant, though, she said, "Right. And I know you chased her in the parking lot, because I saw you."

"You saw me? I didn't see you."

"Yes, you did. You just didn't know it. I fell over that parking bump, and people were trying to help me."

"That was you?" I remembered Tara running up to the group of kids looking down at something, some of them bending or crouching. "That was when you hurt your foot?"

She nodded. "I also know there's no way you stomped out of the gym and immediately attacked Tara. What I don't know is what really happened."

Stomped? I didn't *stomp*.

I decided to let that go for now. Instead, I told her about going to my car that night. "Sounds stupid now, but I thought it was a monster or something. When it ran toward the gym, I wanted to warn everybody. Then, when I saw it was just Tara, I wanted to see what was wrong and help her."

"That makes sense." She looked at the clock again, then down at the email. "Okay, this bit about you joking about things like rape. I'd guess whoever wrote this got it from Rob or Kevin."

I took the page back. It was getting more crumpled all the time, and the margins had chocolate chip fingerprints. "This isn't true either."

"But there's a little truth, isn't there? Like with the parking lot, and me, and you watching Tara. Everything's partly true. That makes it harder."

She was right.

I sighed. "The guys—Rob and Kevin—used to joke about me being a Viking, and how that meant raping and pillaging. They said

143

something about that when we were talking about, well, about Tara. The first day she came." This was embarrassing. "I laughed, but I didn't think it was funny."

"Then why did you laugh?"

How could I explain? I'd felt stupid enough telling Jeff. It made me sound like such a wimp, especially since Lovejoy seemed so sure of herself and her own ideas. I couldn't imagine her doing or saying anything just to fit in. She was too honest.

I opened my mouth.

"Forget it. That's just something people do." She pulled the paper out of my hand. "So, who do you think wrote this, and why?"

"Alex White," I said promptly. "He likes Tara, and he was there both times. In the parking lot, and when she had that meltdown at her locker. He basically accused me then."

She shook her head. "Not his style. I know Alex, and I can't imagine him doing this. He'd confront you to your face. He wouldn't sneak." She rattled the paper. "This has a *mean* feeling to it."

"How about that guy Bingo? No, never mind."

Bingo was the meanest, crudest guy I could think of, and he definitely thought I'd attacked Tara. But he hadn't seen anything wrong with that. Except he thought I should've picked a better place to do it.

Across the room, Lovejoy's purse burst into a series of drum rolls punctuated by a staccato voice shouting, "Hey, boss lady!" I jumped up and brought it to her.

"That's my mom's ringtone." She pulled out her phone and flipped it open. "Hi, Mom. Sure. Sure. Okay, see you in a minute." A high-pitched squawk came through the phone. "Love you, too, Tootsie Pop."

She hung up and tucked the phone back inside. "She's on her way. Five minutes, and she wants me ready to go when she gets here. She's got things to do." She held up her fingers to make quote marks around the last three words.

"You call your mom Tootsie Pop?"

"What?" She laughed. "No, that's my dog. She's a shih tzu."

Whatever. "I could take you home, you know," I said.

"With that eye?" She scooted forward and reached for her crutches. "Have you tried driving yet? I got a black eye once when I was a kid. Walking wasn't bad, but when I tried to ride my bike, I was all over the place. Driving would be even worse."

I hadn't thought of that.

When I helped Lovejoy into her old duffel coat, I somehow got her hand through a rip in the armhole lining and almost knocked her over. Intent on protecting her bad ankle, I grabbed her around the waist and squashed her against me. While I tried to figure out how to let go without dropping her, she giggled into my shirt. It tickled.

"Whoa, no wonder you're getting a reputation." She struggled upright, pulling her crutches into place. "You're not safe to be around."

Not safe. Lovejoy had no idea how important those words could be. She was laughing, but *not safe* was exactly what Tara believed about me, and for her there was nothing funny in that. With DID, not being safe was the worst thing you could be.

"I do have an idea," Lovejoy said as I walked her to the door. "I mean, about who might've written this. But I'm not going to say until I'm sure."

"Who?"

Her curls bounced as she shook her head.

"But you don't think it's Alex."

"He's a good guy, Bank. I think you'd be terrific friends."

As I opened the door, a black Subaru pulled up to the curb.

"That's her," she said. "Oh, I forgot. Please tell your mom thanks for the cookies. They were unbelievable."

"I'll walk you out."

On the sidewalk, a fat dog on a leash stopped to bark at the car. In the back seat, Lovejoy's dog—Tootsie Roll?—yipped back and scrabbled its claws against the window. The gray-haired woman walking the dog stared at Lovejoy and me. I hadn't thought about how bizarre we must look. Lovejoy on crutches, me with one eye bruised and swollen partly shut.

I smiled, trying to look peaceful, but Lovejoy turned sharply toward me. "You do that again," she said, "and I'll black your other eye!"

"*What?*"

"Sorry," she murmured. "Couldn't resist." She kept her face stern, but her brown eyes sparkled as the woman jerked the leash and hurried past, glancing fearfully back at us. "I hope that isn't anybody you know."

"That's my grandma. She lives in the next block."

Lovejoy's mouth dropped open.

"Not really." I grinned. "Sorry. Couldn't resist."

For a second, I thought she really *was* going to black my other eye.

25

Disloyal

Monday morning, I ate breakfast with Cry. Not a great way to start the day.

She came out mostly to look at my eye. She kept squinting at it, complaining that she wished she could see the colors better. Mom had told me it was important to love and appreciate all of the alters, but Cry got my vote for least favorite. Every time she came out, she hinted about needing glasses and tried to make us feel guilty because we wouldn't get them for her.

Too bad both she and Fighter hadn't integrated instead of Libby and Hope.

Halfway through breakfast, the phone on the kitchen counter rang. Cry and I looked at each other. "Must be Dad," I said. He checked in every morning when he was on a business trip.

No question about who should get it. I reached for another pancake as Cry went inside to get Meredith.

Mom came out blinking in surprise. Cry must have given her a pretty good shove.

"Dad," I mumbled with my mouth full, pointing my fork at the phone.

She went over and frowned at the caller ID, then picked up. "Hello? Oh. Oh, of course. How are you?" After a long pause, she nodded. "I think that's a good idea. I'll ask him." She smiled. "No, you're probably right. I'll *tell* him."

She hung up, still smiling. "That was Lovejoy. I like that girl."

"Lovejoy? What's up?"

"She and her mother are taking you to school. They'll pick you up in fifteen minutes. She doesn't think you're safe to drive yet because of your eye." She came over to study my face. "It's not as swollen now, but I think she's right. Let's give it another day or two."

I huffed around a mouthful of pancake, but my gut reaction was relief. The bruising looked worse than it felt, and I could see just fine, but today it would be great to walk in with a friend. Especially Lovejoy.

Aha. Maybe that was her real motivation for coming to get me.

I watched Mom fixing herself a cup of hot tea. She looked peaceful. Unworried. If Lovejoy's call had a double motive—to keep me from driving before it was safe *and* give moral support on my first morning back among the hyenas—she wouldn't mention the second motive on the phone. I'd warned her Mom didn't know the full story behind my black eye, that she thought it had just been an accident. I said I wanted her to keep thinking that way.

"You're sweet, Bank," Lovejoy had said. "It would just worry her, wouldn't it?"

Sweet. That word again. Remembering Jeff's first long email about Rose, I grinned. I'd have to tell him the girl I'd knocked down was now calling me *sweet.*

For the drive to school, I crammed my legs in back with Tootsie Pop, who crouched on the seat and bulged her eyes at me the whole time. I thought about patting her but decided not to. It would be embarrassing if Lovejoy's dog bit me.

The front seat mostly stayed quiet. Lovejoy and her mom both said hello when I climbed in, but not much after that.

I figured they'd had a fight. Probably about me. Yesterday when her mom had picked her up at my house, Lovejoy was supposed to be out front and ready to jump straight into the car. Was that really because her mom had other things to do? Maybe she just didn't want to talk to me.

Or maybe it was the black eye. It did make me look like a thug. For the rest of the ride, I tried to be polite and sociable and show how nonviolent I really was, but I had a feeling my strategy wasn't working.

I was right. The instant her mom drove off after letting us out, Lovejoy turned to me. "I've never seen you act like that, Bank. What were you *doing*?"

"Being smarmy," I said gloomily.

"Smarmy?"

"Sucking up. Toadying."

"Oh." The corners of her mouth curled. "Yeah, you were. Don't do it again, okay?"

Her mom had dropped us off at the front door, which was good for Lovejoy on her crutches. Bad for me, though. I'd much rather have gone the long route from the parking lot. I would take as much time as I could get before I had to face everybody.

As we stepped inside, I half expected to see a gigantic crowd of kids armed with volleyballs, ready to let loose at me. Instead, everyone roamed the halls as usual, laughing, yelling, talking, flirting, banging lockers, poking at each other.

A tube of lip stuff fell out of a girl's purse as she walked by. I said, "Hey, you dropped something," and reached down to pick it up for her.

"Thanks." She took it and went on down the hall. Nobody paid any attention.

This felt just like any other morning.

Lovejoy and I looked at each other. "Good start," she said, turning toward the elevator. "See you at lunch?"

"Yeah. That'd be great."

The Bee came buzzing out of her office and stared up at me, head tipped back to study my black eye. "How do you feel?"

"A lot better. Thanks."

"Hm. Bank, you're excused from P.E. for the week. Your

149

class is still on volleyball, and Coach Summers doesn't want to risk further damage. For now, you'll go to the library for extra study time."

Great news. Asking to get out of P.E. would have qualified as running away. But this had been handed to me like a late Christmas present. Go, Rudolph.

I grinned. It also meant I could get to biology faster all week. Get a few minutes with Lovejoy before the bell rang.

As the morning went on, nobody hit me or accused me of attacking Tara. But nobody talked to me, either. People looked at my bruised face, either openly or with a quick side glance, then away. No eye contact. I'd see a group of kids staring at me and talking, but when they saw I'd noticed them, they'd look some other direction. One girl made an ugly face at me, but that was normal for her.

I spent so much time in giant cooked noodle configuration, it almost stopped bothering me. Probably a good thing, since I might have to live the rest of my life this way.

Just before third-hour math, I saw Max and Rajid. They were several yards ahead of me, about to walk through the door, when somebody yelled my name from behind.

I turned. "Hey, Trevor. What's up?"

"About that tennis racquet I loaned you." His voice came out so loud, people around us turned to look. I braced myself, figuring he wanted his racquet back since I was such a creep and didn't deserve to use it. Instead, he said, "It's yours. If you want it."

"Seriously? Why?"

He shrugged. "It's a good racquet. You're a good player, and you ought to have a decent racquet. I want you to have it."

"Wow, thanks. Are you sure you—"

"Let's play some this week. I'll see if I can get an indoor court, and maybe we can set up some doubles. You okay to play with your eye like that?"

"Sure. No problem."

"Great." He punched me on the arm. "I'll let you know."

150

Walking into math class, I spotted an empty desk at the back. I scooted it against the wall so I could stretch out my legs. A couple of kids who'd been in the hall and heard Trevor talking turned to look at me. They actually made eye contact. I didn't want to push my luck by smiling at them, but I didn't want to look hostile either. As a compromise, I borrowed Viking Clone's NBR face.

Very useful.

Since half of the class was still confused about what we'd worked on last week, Mrs. Adams had us do problems at our desks so she could be around for questions. She might not be popular, but she was a good teacher. She wouldn't just move on and leave people dangling. I finished, checked through my paper, and still had plenty of time left while she worked with the danglers.

Time to think about other things, like what Trevor had just done. Something about it had hit me wrong. Giving me the racquet was an amazingly generous thing for him to do, especially right now, but…

I was frowning, trying to pin down exactly what had bothered me, when Mrs. Adams loomed over me and snapped out, "Bank!"

Was frowning illegal? I looked up defensively.

"I want you to help Janessa here." She rapped on the desk of the girl to my left. "She has herself so tangled up, it'll take the rest of the hour to straighten her out."

As Mrs. Adams walked off, Janessa and I looked at each other. I tried a smile. She looked away.

"Um, I'm going to scoot my desk over a little." I figured I'd better warn her, or she might think I was attacking her. "So we can see better, you know."

I edged cautiously over a few inches and picked up her paper. Wow. Mrs. Adams was right. "Okay," I said. "I think it'll make more sense if we start back here. The book makes this part sound more complicated than it really is."

It took a lot of work, but by the end of the hour, Janessa was getting most of the answers right. And she was actually smiling and talking to me.

"Wow, thanks," she said, as the bell rang and I shoved my desk back. "And thanks for not acting like I'm stupid. With math, it's just like my mind goes blank. I don't know why."

"You're in my Spanish class. You're great at that."

"I love languages. I want to teach ESL. English as a Second Language, you know." She picked up her book bag. "Thanks a lot, Bank."

By the time I got my things together and looked around, Max and Rajid had gone. Disappointing, but not surprising. When I'd thought about it over the weekend, Rajid's attitude Friday afternoon hadn't exactly oozed friendliness. After he and Max talked to me at my locker that morning, they must've seen the email and changed their minds about me.

I couldn't blame them. After all, they hardly knew me. But it still bothered me, even more than Rob and Kevin's disloyalty.

Walking to the cafeteria by myself, I puzzled over that. It seemed backwards. Getting dumped by longtime friends should hit you way harder than when new ones did it. I thought about Jeff's email. *Bro, you can do a lot better than Rob and Kev. Rob used to be okay, but now he's all about himself. Kev's just Kev.*

Maybe that explained it. That friendship came out of the past, out of who I used to be. The tennis guys were me, now.

Or at least I'd thought so.

26

Loyal

Whack!

They must've been waiting for me just inside the cafeteria door. The blow landed on my shin, right where I'd clobbered it on the toilet the week before. It hurt like fury. Grabbing at my leg with one hand, I flung up the other to protect my head.

"I'm *sorry*, Bank. Are you okay?"

Lovejoy, brown eyes big and horrified, stood beside the door with a crutch dangling from one hand. "That got out of control. I just wanted to get your attention. Did I hurt you?"

Come on, manly-man. Suck it up. "No. No, I'm okay." I blinked hard. "Um, so, where do you want to sit?"

I'd already considered the possibilities. We couldn't sit at Lovejoy's usual table with Alex and Tara. And the way Max and Rajid had acted lately, the tennis table was out, too.

She patted my book bag. "Did you bring your lunch? Good. Me, too. Come on."

"We can't go to the computer lab," I said, as we both limped away from the cafeteria. "You know The Bee's going to check there every lunch hour for the next fifty years."

"I know. I've got a better place."

She turned down the short hall that led to the art room. "Chuck said this would be okay. He's here working on a painting, so he can be our official chaperone. But he won't bother us."

"Who's Chuck?"

"My art teacher. Chuck Durango." She shook her head. "You

153

don't know anything about my world, do you?"

She was right. My mind had been too stuck on myself.

"Why do you call him Chuck?" I lowered my voice as we walked in. "Mrs. Adams would knock my head off if I called her anything but Mrs. Adams. I don't think she even *has* a first name."

"Art's different. It's not as formal." She dropped her book bag on a smeary-looking table and sat down. "Hi, Chuck, we're here. This is Bank."

A bearded guy peered from behind an easel in a corner of the big, messy room. He waved a paintbrush at me. I waved back, feeling awkward.

"Wow, he really looks like an artist." I sat down across from her. "Like he should be in Paris or something."

She laughed. "All part of the performance. People in this world like to act the part. They can be pretty fake."

"You're not."

"No, I'm not. Some are, some aren't." She dumped her lunch onto the table. An apple went rolling, and I caught it just as it tipped over the side.

"You might want to wash that," I said. "This table's dirty."

"That's not dirt. It's art." She took the apple from me. "Actually, it's mostly ink. We're into printmaking now. Lithography." She held out her hands. "I look like a car mechanic, don't I? The ink gets under your nails, and then the acid you use to clean things up ruins your skin. Chuck says you can tell a true artist by his ugly hands. I must be a true artist."

"Your hands aren't ugly. They're…"

I wasn't sure what word to use. Her hands weren't pretty, not with the short, stained fingernails and rough skin. But I liked them. She watched me, smiling.

"Interesting," I said finally. "They have character. Like you."

"Mm. Right." She bit into the apple. "You'd better eat, or we'll run out of time. The last thing we need is another trip to the office for a late pass."

I pulled out a peanut butter sandwich. "You know, Lovejoy, I don't want to mess things up for you."

Her crutches, propped against the table, slid sideways. She caught them and reached over to drop them on the floor. "What do you mean, mess things up?"

"With your friends. You should be sitting with them in the cafeteria right now. If hanging out with me is going to mess things up with your friends—"

"Bank, shut up. Please."

I grinned. Sometimes expressions of loyalty don't come in fancy phrases. "Yes, ma'am."

When my first sandwich had taken the edge off my hunger, I decided it was time to get into her world. "So, what's lithography? I know 'litho' means stone."

"Really? I didn't know that. But you're right. We draw on those slabs of Bavarian limestone. See?" She pointed toward what looked like thick patio flagstones lined up along one counter. "I'll show you mine later."

I tried to listen while she explained the printing process. But I kept getting distracted, watching her talk and thinking how fun and full of life she was. Her lips looked soft, nice to kiss. Lovejoy wasn't gorgeous like Tara. She went way beyond that. She was—

"What?" she demanded.

"What do you mean, what?"

"You're staring at me like I have ink on my face or something."

"I was just thinking how great you are," I said honestly. There had to be a better word than "great," but I hadn't come up with it yet.

"Oh." Her cheeks and the tip of her nose went pink. "Oh, well. Your turn to talk. Tell me what's been going on today."

"Not much. Except for some girl whacking me with a crutch. Oh, yeah, and this weird thing happened with Trevor." I told her about the episode in the hall.

She peeled strings off a stick of celery. "So, what's weird?"

"Well, for one thing, it's too much. I went online last week to see what racquets cost, and I couldn't believe how much this one's worth. It's not new, but it's in great shape." I grinned. "I've been a lot more careful with it ever since. If I broke it or lost it, I'd never be able to pay him back."

"And now it's yours."

"I know. And I've been thinking. It's weird enough for Trevor to give it to me, when he hardly even knows me. But what's weirder is the *way* he did it. In front of everybody like that. Like he's showing off, saying, 'Hey, look what a great guy I am!'"

She nodded. "You think that was out of character?"

"Definitely. And he was talking so loud, people were turning around to look. I'd expect him to do it like it was no big deal, the same way he loaned the racquet to me in the first place."

"Quietly. So nobody else would know." Her curly smile broadened.

"Yeah, exactly. What's so funny?"

"Come on, we've got to get going." She reached for her crutches. "Just think about it, Bank. You're smart. I'll bet you can figure out why he did it that way."

I did, but it took me most of the day. The answer didn't hit me until after sixth hour, when Lovejoy and I went to our lockers together. On the way, she kept calling out to people she knew, and they always turned to look. Sometimes when they smiled back, I got included.

Aha.

Just like Lovejoy, coming with me to school this morning and sticking with me as much as she could after that, Trevor had a reason for what he'd done. And I was almost sure his motive was the same as hers.

They were on my team. And they wanted people to know it.

27

Team

After school, Lovejoy and I waited just inside the front door for her mom to show up. "I should be okay to drive tomorrow," I said. "Want me to pick you up in the morning?"

"I'd like that. That'd be cool." Her smile curled. "You might need your car, though."

I started to say, "Well, duh," but caught myself. "Well, yeah," I said instead. I was learning.

Her smile curled higher. "Remember? Coach Summers took you to the hospital, and your mom drove you home from there. Your car's still in the school parking lot."

"The Prizm stayed here all weekend? Oh, cripes."

There was no way my car hadn't been vandalized. As of last Friday, kids would've considered it their patriotic duty to slash my tires and key the paint, not to mention jumping on the hood and smashing volleyballs through the windows. I would be without transportation for the rest of my life. Which meant until Thursday, since Dad would kill me as soon as he got back in town.

I pulled out my keys. "Would your mom wait? I might still need a ride."

"Sure. Just call me, either way." She held up her phone. "You've got my number."

Nodding distractedly, I bent toward her upturned face. Her eyes widened. I got halfway to the parking lot before I realized why.

This time I hadn't just imagined kissing those curly lips. I'd actually done it.

"Whoa." I broke stride for a second, then kept going. With basic survival at stake, romance would have to wait.

Dodging the crazy traffic in the school lot, I tried to remember where I'd parked last Friday. I couldn't see the Prizm anywhere. Maybe someone had stolen it. Or the school had towed it away as an abandoned vehicle, which meant paying big bucks to get it back.

A silver SUV gunned backward and took off, tires squealing, black smoke spewing from its exhaust pipe. I waved the noxious fog away from my face and squinted. On the other side of the empty spot sat my car.

I ran over and patted the roof. The Prizm looked dirtier than when I'd parked it there three and a half days ago, but that was all. It started up right away, too. I couldn't believe it. Nobody had ripped out wires, siphoned gas, or dumped sugar in the tank.

I blew out my breath and sagged against the seat. Then I grabbed my phone.

What a life. That evening, I summed it up for Jeff in three sentences.

To: jeffers@moondog.com
From: bankrobber@cvc.org
Subject:

Hey Jefferson. Trevor gave me a tennis racquet that could pay off the national debt. I kissed Lovejoy for the first time. Everyone else hates me and wants to beat me to death with volleyballs.

Later $

Next morning, I left early in case I had trouble finding Lovejoy's house. I got there ten minutes ahead of schedule, which turned out to be the best thing I could've done. Her mom was hugely impressed with my hyper-punctuality. She actually smiled when she opened the door.

"Lovejoy's not quite ready," she said. "She isn't an early bird like you."

Even Tootsie Pop warmed up. She still bulged her eyes at me, but this time it almost looked friendly.

I'd washed and vacuumed the Prizm for the great event, clearing out all the junk that had collected in the back. As we pulled away from the curb, Lovejoy's crutches slid and clunked against each other on the back seat. I looked at her sitting beside me, exactly as I'd pictured—how long ago? Must've been last Wednesday, on my way to Viking Clone's. Less than a week. At the time, it had seemed impossible.

Of course, I'd started by daydreaming about Tara sitting there instead.

A flick of guilt popped up. Partly because the dream had included someone besides Lovejoy, but mostly because I hadn't thought about Tara's meltdown except for how it affected *me*. I had no idea how she was doing.

The heater was still blowing cool air. I turned it off. "Hey, did you see Tara at school yesterday?"

"Wondered when you were going to ask about her." Lovejoy yawned. Definitely not a morning person, which might explain why her half of the front seat had been so quiet the day before. "No, she wasn't at school. She didn't answer when I called, either."

"Huh." That didn't sound good.

"I thought she must not know about that email and what people were saying about you. Otherwise she'd do something. You know, tell the truth." She blinked and ran her fingers through her curly hair. "So I went over to her house last night."

"You did? Did you talk to her?"

"Yeah. It was really sad, though. She was so *different*. Oh." She turned to stare at me. "Is that what you were talking about in The Bee's office? About Tara having some kind of disorder?"

"Maybe. What was she like?"

"Scared, I think. She wouldn't look at me. She just sat there with her head down and her shoulders kind of hunched."

So, the confident supermodel had gone inside. Not integrated, probably, but hiding.

I paused at a four-way stop, then went on. "Did she say anything?"

Lovejoy shook her head. "By the time I left, I wasn't sure if she even understood what I'd told her about you. I thought maybe she was on drugs. But you think that was actually a different person?"

"Not exactly a person. The alters each have their own name, and they're different ages and all that, but…"

I stopped talking to concentrate on the car in front of me. It showed all the signs of a new driver, including the nervous parent shifting around in the passenger seat and a lot of jerky and unnecessary braking. The last thing I needed was to rear-end them and hurt Lovejoy's other leg.

"It's kind of hard to explain," I said, changing lanes.

"Why do you know so much about—what's it called? And what does it stand for again?"

"DID. Dissociative Identity Disorder. People used to call it Multiple Personality Disorder, but they changed the name since the alters really aren't personalities. Did you ever see any of those old movies, like *The Three Faces of Eve*, or *Sybil*?"

"No. Never heard of them."

I passed the new driver, keeping an eye out in case the car drifted into my lane. We were less than a block from school. Maybe Lovejoy would forget she had also asked me why—

"Why do you know so much about it? Hey, look, that's Anna Pidderco. I heard she got her permit." She waved, and I sped out of the way as the girl waved back and her car swerved toward us. "Anyway, why do you know so much about DID?"

She hadn't forgotten.

I took a deep breath. "Can I tell you later?"

In the silence, I could feel her staring at me.

"Sure," she said finally. "Lunch again? Let's just meet in the art room this time."

"Sounds good." I didn't want another crutch across the shin in the cafeteria doorway. I pulled up in front of the school to drop her off. "Hang on. I'll get your door. And your crutches."

I had the perfect scenario all worked up for a morning kiss. I'd given it a *lot* of thought. When she swung her legs out of the Prizm, I leaned down and handed her the crutches. "I dreamed about you last night," I said. "You know, about kissing you."

"Dream all you want. That's the only kind of kiss you're going to get for a while." She looked up and made a face. "Sorry, that didn't come out right. It's just that I don't want to move too fast, Bank. Most people do, and I see what it does to them. I want us to get to really *know* each other."

How could I argue with that?

I sure wanted to.

"I liked your kiss." Lovejoy took hold of my arm. "I liked it a lot. I probably shouldn't say that, because it sounds like I'm just playing games. But I'm not." Her grip tightened. "I want more for us than that. I don't want to be like everybody else."

As if that was even possible. But it helped.

A little.

The morning went basically the way it had the day before. Not great, not terrible. At lunchtime, I went to the art room and got my second big disappointment of the day. Trevor sat across from Lovejoy, talking intently.

My ribs took a jab of something that might be jealousy. I hoped not. I sure didn't want to turn into one of those obnoxious possessive boyfriends.

"Hey, Trevor," I said, trying to sound friendly.

Lovejoy gave me a look that probably meant I'd overdone it. *Smarmy.*

"Hey, Bank." He stood up and reached across the table to smack my shoulder. "I wanted to talk to you. Lovejoy said this would be okay. It won't take long."

"Sure."

He sat down again. Lovejoy smiled as I pulled a chair close to hers. Her arm felt warm against mine.

Watching us, Trevor smiled, too. "I just wanted to tell you guys about something that happened to me a couple of years ago." He waved a hand at her. "Go ahead and eat, Lovejoy."

I pulled a sandwich out of my book bag. Why did everyone keep telling her to eat, when I was the hungry one?

Lovejoy peeled off a note taped to her apple. "Oh, that's right." She made a face. "I have a doctor appointment this afternoon, Bank. I won't be in sixth hour, and I won't need a ride home. Mom's picking me up."

"Oh." Major disappointment number three. Everything good had just emptied out of the afternoon.

"Want to play some tennis after school?" Trevor asked. "I

have an indoor court reserved. I was going to practice serves on my own, but I'd rather play."

"I don't have my racquet here. Your racquet."

"*Your* racquet," he said. "Don't worry. I always have extras."

"Yeah, sure. I'd like to."

"Great." His expression went serious. "Anyway, I'll make this fast. Two years ago, I made the tennis team. I was just a freshman, but I was already a better player than the older guys on the team." He shrugged. "That's just the way it was, and I honestly didn't have the big head about it. I just loved to play."

I nodded.

"I wasn't that great in school, though. Especially math." He tapped his head. "I've always had trouble with math. So, just before midterms, I said something during practice, and this guy offered to tutor me. Junior on the team, really sharp guy named Kent. He was a good tutor, and he worked me hard. I aced my math midterm. I knew *everything* on that test. Man, was I happy."

He glanced at Lovejoy, then back at me. "My paper came back with a big fat F. They thought I'd cheated."

"Wow." I set down my sandwich. "Didn't you tell them?"

"Of course. They didn't believe me. Especially since while I was in class taking the test, they got an anonymous tip that I had the answer sheet in my locker. They checked. It was there."

"Oh." Lovejoy's face came alive with sympathy. "He did it, didn't he? That guy Kent?"

That didn't make sense to me. "Why would *he* do it? He was helping Trevor."

She gave me the look again, but this time she was smiling. "Bank, you're just too nice."

"Anybody could've put it there," Trevor said. "I had this impossible lock, so I never locked it. I still don't know for sure. But Kent had been the hot guy on the courts till I came along, which was why I thought it was especially cool of him to help me. They kicked me off the team, said I had to wait two years before I could try out

163

again. Nobody believed me. Nobody backed me up."

He shrugged. "I probably should've pushed it, but it didn't seem worth the effort. I didn't want to be with a bunch of guys who'd believe the worst of me. None of them knew me all that well, but I thought they knew me better than to think I was a liar and a cheat."

That felt familiar.

"So, anyway. I waited my two years. Now I'm back on the team." He looked at me. "And now you're where I was. I don't think you're the kind of guy to do what they're saying you did to that girl. Are you?"

My face heated up, but I tried to keep my eyes steady. "No. I'm not."

He'd been serious this whole time, but now he grinned. "Yeah, Lovejoy has better taste than that."

"Thanks." My voice sounded thick. I cleared my throat. "I wish somebody had, you know, stood up for you."

"Me, too. You know, except for getting kicked off the team, it wasn't such a big deal. A lot of kids cheat, and they mostly just thought I was stupid to get caught. But the tennis. That *was* a big deal. I don't want that to happen to you."

"I'm not on the team."

"I know." He scooted his chair back and stood. "And if Coach hears about this and thinks you did it, you won't be. Ever."

164

28

Telling

Trevor and I played until Coach finished his paperwork and wanted to lock up the gym. As we left the courtroom, I picked up the Barbie head and gave Ed's bronze foot a good smack.

"Thanks, Trevor. This was great." I handed the head to him. "I haven't played in—wow, I guess it's been a week."

"I could tell. Now that your eye's better, you ought to play every day. You had some good momentum going, but you've gone backwards."

I didn't say anything.

"What's the matter?" He shot me a challenging look. "It's the truth."

"It's not that. It's just, I can't. Not unless *you*'ll play every day." I could tell he still didn't get it. Sounding like a pathetic little kid, I said, "I don't have anybody else to play with."

"What about Max? Or Raj? I thought you guys were playing. They need the practice, too."

"They haven't talked to me since that email. The one about Tara, I mean. I guess they believed it."

Coach's voice echoed across the empty gym. "Come on, guys. Out. I have a life, even if you don't."

"Wish I could tell you," Trevor said as we walked to the parking lot. "But I don't know what's going on in those guys' heads. I haven't seen much of them lately."

"I shouldn't have said anything. I didn't mean to whine."

He laughed. "If I hear anything, I'll let you know."

165

After dinner, trudging up the stairs to my room, I thought, *Coach was sure right about me not having a life.*

Except for Lovejoy. And after her doctor appointment, she had a paper to write and two tests to study for, all due tomorrow. I'd asked her if we could do homework together tonight, but she said no. "I just can't study with other people. I know everybody else does, but I can't. I get too distracted."

I dumped my book bag onto my desk. Tonight I had a pile of schoolwork, too. Usually I stayed on top of it—probably because I didn't have a life—but lately I'd fallen off. I'd forgotten all about the eight-page paper I had to write about *Lord of the Flies*, and now I'd have to push to get it done. I could do ten pages of math faster than one of English. I like words, but they're more complicated than numbers.

First, I checked my email.

Nothing from Jeff, which didn't surprise me. Lately I was lucky to hear from him at all. I didn't wish bad news on his romantic life, but it would be nice if he and Rose backed off a little so he had a few minutes for me. I'd started to think our lifetime friendship might fizzle out after just a month apart.

My hand, cupped over the mouse, ready to open a blank document and start my English paper, slid across the mouse pad Jeff had given me. *There is a friend who sticks closer than a brother.*

Yeah, right.

I stopped. Yeah. Right. That *was* right. This was one friend I wasn't giving up on, which meant I had to make an effort even if he didn't. The mouse scurried back to the most recent email from Jeff and clicked on *reply*.

As I started typing, I heard the doorbell.

Lovejoy? Stopping by to report on her foot? Since I'd won her mom's approval as a fellow early bird, she might've been willing to bring her by after the appointment. Maybe I could talk her into letting Lovejoy stay for dinner. Mom would definitely say yes. And then maybe Lovejoy would change her mind about studying with me.

Not likely, though. When Lovejoy developed an opinion, she stuck to it.

As the front door opened, I went into the hall to listen. I heard the murmur of voices, but nobody called up to me. Must be one of Mom's friends. I went back to my computer.

To: jeffers@moondog.com
From: bankrobber@cvc.org
Subject:

Hey Jefferson. How's it going? Nothing new here. The way it's been going lately that's probably a good thing. Lovejoy wants to know why I know so much about DID, so tomorrow at lunch I'm going to tell her about my mom. She should do okay with it. Hope so anyway.

Later $

Not much of an effort, maybe. But better than nothing.

Wednesday morning, Mom seemed quieter than usual. I didn't think much of it. My mind was focused on getting out the door, since I wanted to pick up Lovejoy early enough to make more points with her mom. That was one person I definitely wanted on my team.

This time, though, I barely got my car door open before Lovejoy came out and down her porch steps. She looked a lot more awake than the day before, smiling so her whole face seemed full of light. I was so busy looking at her eyes and mouth, it took a few seconds to realize what else was different.

"Hey!" I shouted. "Way to go."

She put a finger to her lips and pointed at the quiet houses on each side, but she was still smiling.

I went around and opened the passenger door. "How's it feel?"

"Terrific." She slid in. "You wouldn't *believe* how good it feels."

Lovejoy had her ankle strapped, with orders to keep it elevated as much as she could. But she was now officially off crutches. The doctor had said it would be better for her foot if she stayed on them another week, but she'd had some tingling in her hands. He was afraid of possible nerve damage.

"I promised him I'd be careful." Her smile curled deeper. "I would've promised *anything*."

That worried me. "But you will be careful?"

"I will. I keep my promises, and I don't want to get stuck using crutches again. And I definitely don't want to ruin my hands." She waggled her fingers. "They may be ugly, but I like them."

The funny thing was, hardly anybody noticed. You go to school with a gigantic zit or a new haircut—or no crutches—and everybody's too busy thinking about themselves to pay attention. Today, my black eye hardly got any looks either. I still belonged in the conhead category, but if nothing else happened to stir up the rumors, by next month I'd be invisible again.

That sounded great.

"Hey, what's going on with Mandy?" I held her arm as we walked upstairs. "I never see the two of you together now. Did I mess up your friendship?"

"*You*'d probably think so, but I don't. I think Rob is the problem."

Her expression reminded me of Mandy's during the Bank-being-a-jerk disaster, when she'd snapped, "Lovejoy was sure wrong about *you*," and marched off down the hall. That had been a bad moment for me. I got a twinge of sympathy for Rob. These women could be fierce when it came to their friends.

"He micromanages her," she said. "And since *he* doesn't like you, she's not allowed to either."

"I thought it was the other way around."

She shook her head. "Mandy was mad at you at first, but she got over it as soon as I did. She's not a grudge kind of person. It's Rob's who's still against you."

This was news.

We got to Lovejoy's locker first. I held her book bag while she hung up her coat.

"Are you sure?" I asked. "I thought Rob was just mad at me because Mandy was because of you." I'd forgotten how ridiculous the whole thing sounded. Kindergarten drama. "Rob was okay with me before that."

She pulled out a book and banged the door shut. "Mandy and I haven't talked since Friday. We kind of had a fight about you."

"Oh, great."

"It's not your fault, so stop it. Actually, I think she's getting tired of Rob. He's really selfish, Bank. I don't understand why you were friends with him."

"Habit."

"I'm serious."

"So am I."

She laughed. "You're so good for me. Most people let me run all over them."

"Thanks for the warning." As we moved to my locker, I couldn't help but glance at Tara's. I pointed. "Hey, her lock's gone."

"I heard she's out for good. Either home school or private school."

"Because of me."

"*Not* because of you. Honestly, Bank. If the ceiling fell on my head right this second, you'd blame yourself because I would've

169

been somewhere else if it wasn't for you. You try to take care of everybody, but you can't. Nobody can."

This might've been annoying, except that she looked so earnest.

"You're pontificating," I said. "That's a peccadillo."

Her smile curled. "You say the sweetest things."

We met for lunch at the art table again. I thought the room was empty, but when Lovejoy called, "Hi, Chuck," the bearded face peeked out from behind a big canvas on the easel. He waved his brush at me again.

I lowered my voice. "Was he here yesterday?"

She nodded. "He's quiet. I think sometimes he goes to sleep back there."

Lovejoy was great about my mom. I knew she would be, but it was still a relief. I told her everything. I even told her about being born in the mental hospital, and about Viking Clone. She listened intently and asked some good questions.

"Wow. That explains a lot," she said at last.

"Like what?"

Her cheeks and the tip of her nose went pink. She picked up a tangerine and gave a lot of attention to peeling it. "Like your fascination with Tara."

Pieces of rind dropped onto the table. She nudged them into a design with one sticky finger. "You're so used to watching out for your mom, but now she doesn't need it as much. You're not even supposed to anymore." She looked up. "Then along comes this cute girl in the exact same situation, and there you are. You have somebody to take care of again."

Amazing. I wondered if Lovejoy had ever thought about a career in counseling. She sure had the right instincts. Maybe she could do art therapy.

"You know, my mom's an artist." I looked around the room, thinking how much Mom would love to have a place like this to work. "She's really good. A lot of people with DID are artists. Creative, imaginative people are the most likely to dissociate."

"That makes sense." She flipped a strip of tangerine peel at me. It hit my shoulder and dropped to the floor. "You changed the subject, though."

I was honestly surprised. My thought processes had been logical enough, but I hadn't taken Lovejoy along with me. Or maybe she hadn't let herself be taken along. She was sticking to the point.

"Tara, you mean?" I picked up my sandwich. "I guess you're right. I wish I could've helped her, but all I did was scare her."

I'd even wondered about the penny I put in Tara's jacket pocket. After all my years of experience with Mom, I should've known better. For all I knew, finding that penny could have triggered some memory and led to her meltdown.

Probably not, but it had been a stupid thing to do.

"Well, *I* wish she hadn't quit school," Lovejoy said. "I wanted her to come back and tell everybody you never attacked her. Now they'll think you did and that's why she left."

I shrugged. "I'm already old news. Something else will happen, and they'll forget about me."

"Unless the something else happens to you," she said.

29

Progress

"Oh, my *goodness*." From behind her desk at The Doors, Tiffany gawked at me. That was the only word for it. *Gawked.* "I always wondered. Now I know."

"Know what?"

"Bank, you've *got* to be related to Dr. Kind."

"You mean the black eye?"

She snickered. "I'm sorry. I'm sure it wasn't funny at the time."

Not all that funny now, either. I forced a smile. "Yeah, well, I've wondered about that myself. Sometimes Dr. Kind looks so much like my dad, it's scary."

"Not quite what you want in a therapist, is it?" She pressed the hidden button, and the door to the hall buzzed. "All right, Bank. See you later. I apologize for teasing you."

"Sure. No problem."

At least she didn't ask how I got the black eye, but I could tell she wanted to. I went down the hall and into Viking Clone's waiting room, where I slumped into a chair and scowled at the magazines. I'd been wondering what to talk about today, but I had a feeling my eye would set our direction. Like it or not.

And I didn't like it. Today I didn't like anything about being here.

I'd completely forgotten about this appointment until Lovejoy and I were at our lockers after sixth hour. Then I tried to hurry her so I wouldn't be late, and she made a bad step going down

172

the stairs. She said her ankle was fine. But I could tell it hurt, and she was limping a little when I let her off at her house. Tomorrow she'd probably be back on crutches, and—

The door to the inner sanctum opened. Viking Clone stepped out. Until that instant, I'd forgotten my goal of getting at least one honestly astonished expression out of him.

I got it now.

Not the way I'd planned, but I would take it. My mood made an upward swing. "I'll tell you about mine," I said, "if you tell me about yours."

When we got ourselves settled, Dr Pepper, cows, and all, he said, "All right, Bank. Last week you asked if a client hit me. The answer is yes."

"Whoa." I tried to look surprised. I didn't want him to know Dr. Sam and Mom had already narked on him.

"This client grew up in a family where showing any strong emotion was unacceptable. He'd struggled with anger for years, trying to hide it even from himself." Viking Clone's chair creaked as he leaned back. "When a person lives like that, pressure builds."

"So he blew."

"That's right. He wasn't necessarily angry with *me*. I just happened to be in front of him when he blew."

He smiled wryly and touched his face. Except for faint yellowish patches and a thin red line where the scab had been, his eye looked normal. Good news for me.

"Sometimes," he said, "the blowup is physical like that. Other times it comes out in words, and those can do even more destruction. Knowing how to express your anger appropriately is like a pressure valve. It lets enough out to keep it from exploding."

"How about tennis? Is that a good pressure valve? You know, running around, yelling, whacking the ball."

"Better than some. It doesn't deal with the issues behind the anger, though." He shifted into NBR. "Do you see this as a problem for you?"

173

A month ago, I'd have said *no way*. Now I nodded. "Anybody getting mad scares my mom, so I've always tried not to. Ever. I haven't blown or anything, but I can tell it's kind of popping up more. Me getting mad, I mean."

"Is that what you'd like to talk about?"

"Not today." Since we were trading "how I got my black eye" stories, I figured my real-life version of *Lord of the Flies* should take up the rest of the hour.

"All right. But let me give you this before I forget." He rolled behind his desk, dug in a bottom drawer, and rolled back out with a pamphlet in his hand. "Homework. We'll talk about it next time."

I leaned forward to take it. The front showed a Dr Seuss-type creature with its head tipped back and its mouth wide open. Books, furniture, and little animals hurtled through the air from the force of whatever the creature was screaming. Colorful letters across the top spelled out *How to Get Mad*.

"Hey, that's not bad." I'd have to show it to Lovejoy, see what she thought as an artist.

He nodded. "It's well done."

I dropped the pamphlet on the floor beside my chair. "What I wanted to talk about—well, a lot's been going on." I pointed at my eye. "Like this."

So, I told him what had happened. Usually I could break a story down into its logical steps, short and sweet, but this time I kept backtracking so different parts would make sense. Finally, I stopped and checked on the cows. They looked bored.

I set my Dr Pepper on the floor next to the pamphlet. "Okay, I think I just figured something out."

Viking Clone's eyebrow edged up.

"I'm not crazy," I said. "I don't need you to shrink me. But sometimes it's like I get stuck. Because of my mom, I've always tried to be, well, invisible. It's like the goal is to be safe. And I still want to be safe for Mom. But for me...I don't think that's a good goal."

He nodded.

"But I've been doing it so long, I get sort of stuck doing that. So maybe we could, you know…" I shrugged, embarrassed. I wasn't even making sense.

"That would be fine, Bank." His chair creaked. "In fact, I think you're right on target. Everyone gets stuck at times. It would help if more people realized that about themselves."

Amazing. But he did look happy.

I picked up my Dr Pepper, then set it back down. "First, though, I've got a question. About integration."

He nodded.

"Okay, you know when I talk about Mom, that's Meredith. And I know Mom and Dad are hoping the alters will all integrate so it's only Meredith. Only Mom." I'd thought about this a lot lately. I'd almost asked her several times.

I took a deep breath. "But what if she's just an alter, too?"

When I left The Doors, I looked around for Tara. No maroon Volvo. No slim, pretty figure with dark hair swirling in the cold breeze.

"It wasn't my fault," I said aloud.

Time to get that through my thick head. I could be sad about what had happened to Tara, but I couldn't take on the responsibility. Someone else had broken her in the first place.

I started the car and turned on the heater. Instead of heading home, I pulled out my wallet and found the directions I'd scribbled down two weeks ago.

This qualified as one of those places in life where I'd gotten stuck, but I didn't need Viking Clone. I knew what to do.

As I climbed the stairs to the second-floor apartment, I heard a TV blaring with some kind of sports program. I poked the doorbell. Footsteps vibrated the floor, and the door opened.

"Bank!" Max looked surprised, but not like my being here was a bad thing. "Were we supposed to play today or something?"

"Nope. I just came by."

"Oh, yeah? That's great." He grinned. Behind him, the announcer howled with excitement. Max held out the remote and cut him dead. "Come on in."

It was a nice enough apartment, but it didn't look like a home. The living room looked and smelled more like a guys' locker room. When Max shoved a pile of clothes and blankets into one corner of the sofa and waved for me to sit down on the other side, I tried to act as if I always sat next to other people's dirty underwear.

Max knew better. "Yeah, I know, it stinks," he said cheerfully, dropping into a chair without bothering to move the clothes out of it. "It's just Dad and my brothers and me here. When Mom left last year, we got this place, and both of my brothers moved back in. Mom's got my little sisters, so Dad has to pay child support." He shrugged. "No more money for the dorms."

"They're both in college?"

"Yeah." He pointed at the sofa where I sat. "That's where John sleeps. Most of this garbage is his. He works fulltime and goes to college, so he's never home to do laundry and stuff. Not like he was ever a neat freak anyway."

He jerked a thumb back over his shoulder. "Tyler shares my room. It's pretty bad, too, but at least we can close the door."

Living like this would drive me nuts, but it didn't seem to bother Max. Slouched in his chair, he rambled on in his usual way

176

about something Mrs. Adams had said to him today in class. Then he shifted to a story about a guy on the tennis team. He looked completely at ease—except for his hands, which gripped the arms of the chair.

It bothered him, all right.

He broke off mid-story. "Hey, you want something to drink?"

"No, I've got to get home in a minute. But I wanted to ask you something." I looked at my own hands, balled into fists on my thighs. "It's this thing about Tara. That email that went all over school."

"Oh. Yeah."

"It's just that you guys haven't been, well, as friendly since then. You and Rajid." I swallowed hard, wishing I'd said yes to a drink. "I wanted to know if you believed it. That I did what that email said, I mean."

Max looked as uncomfortable as I felt. "Yeah, well, we wondered at first, sure. But it just didn't sound like you." He shrugged. "I haven't thought about it that much. This detention stuff's a pain in the rear."

"What detention?"

"You didn't know? I thought everybody did." I could see him trying to hang onto his gloomy expression, but the corners of his mouth twitched. He gave up and grinned. "Yeah, well, for Raj's birthday, his weird cousin gave him this whoopee cushion. You know, you sit on it, and it farts?"

I nodded.

"So, anyway, last Friday we swapped it for that pillow in The Bee's chair, the one she uses to make her look big and scary. Man, it was *so* perfect. Same color and everything. Right after we did it, here she comes with these parents. I guess they're checking out the school to see if it's good enough for their perfect little daughter. The Bee sits down and…"

He did a realistic imitation of a long, loud fart. "You could hear it from clear outside her office. Only problem was, we didn't know Raj's cousin had written on it. 'Whoopee birthday, Rajid,' in neat little letters along one side. It took The Bee maybe five seconds to figure that one out."

"So you got detention?"

"Lunchtime and an hour after school. Two weeks, can you believe it? The Bee was really steamed. Plus, Raj's parents grounded him for the whole two weeks. No phone calls, no tennis, nothing. Brutal."

Aha. So that was why they disappeared so fast after math every day. Instead of lunch as usual, they had to eat theirs in the detention room. It also explained Rajid's attitude Friday afternoon when I'd wanted to set up some tennis with him. I just wished he'd told me.

Max thought everybody knew about his detention. I thought everybody was focused on my criminal reputation.

"Hey, Max," I said. "Did you notice Lovejoy Fox isn't on crutches anymore?"

"Huh. When was she on crutches?"

I said it before. You go to school with a gigantic zit or a new haircut—or crutches—and everybody's too busy thinking about themselves to even notice.

30

Crisis

As I left Max's apartment, I called Lovejoy. "How's your ankle?"

"Oh, it's good. Listen, Bank, I was thinking. What if I came over after dinner and helped you work on your paper?"

Ms. Montoya had extended the due date, which was nice of her. But only to the end of the week. Considering how little I had to show for all the time and effort I'd put in last night, I wouldn't be ready to turn it in until the end of the year.

"Seriously?"

"Sure. I love that kind of project. It's a challenge. And after that pile I had for today, I'm pretty much free until next week. And Mom said she'd drive me." I could hear the smile in her voice. "She likes you."

Life was good.

My parents had a no-girls-in-Bank's-room rule, which I'd never had to obey before, since no girl had ever wanted to be in my room. That meant the hassle of unplugging all the cords, bringing my computer downstairs to the dining room table, and setting it up again.

This made me think about getting a laptop, which made me think about getting a job, which made me think about taking Lovejoy out on dates that actually cost money. So far, our times together hadn't exactly been extravagant. Including tonight.

Working on a paper about *Lord of the Flies*. What a romantic guy.

I'd also brought down Viking Clone's pamphlet. As Mom

came in, I slid it under my book. She might be doing better, but she didn't need to see me reading something called *How to Get Mad*.

"I'm going back to my room to read. I might come out later and say hello." She smiled. "This is my last night to read as late as I want. Your dad comes home tomorrow."

"Oh, right. What time's his flight?"

"He's driving, not flying. Probably late afternoon or early evening, but it could be any time."

I looked at the tangled mess I'd made of the dining room. I'd planned to leave it until after school tomorrow, but not now. Annoying Dad first thing after a long trip wasn't a good idea.

Lovejoy had told me her mom would drop her off at seven. At seven-thirteen, I called her cell phone. She didn't answer. I tried a couple more times. Still no answer.

She was more than half an hour late when she called to say they were on their way. By then, my imagination had her unconscious in the ICU, on a ventilator, with a two percent chance of making it through the night.

"I'm sorry," she said the instant I opened the door. "I *hate* being late. Were you worried?"

"Nah. Not really." I shepherded her into the house. "Here, give me your coat."

She handed it over. "Bank, listen. Rob wrote that email."

"What e—" I stopped.

She nodded. "I thought it might be Rob, but tonight Mandy told me for sure. That's why I'm so late. She came over at six, and we've been talking all this time."

"Wow." The word slid off my tongue, slow and thick. It made me think of Kevin drawling, "*Dude.*" Was he in on this, too?

My hands fumbled as I hung up her coat and shut the closet door. "Come on." I turned away. "Computer's in the dining room."

"Are you...don't you want to hear about it?"

"I have to do this paper. It's due Friday. I've got to get it done."

180

"But, Bank—"

All of a sudden, it was like being back at the gym that night when she told me the crutches and leg brace were just a joke. Only worse. Much worse. Fury ballooned inside me, huge, hot, full, too much and too strong to hold. I felt my mouth shaking, trying to stay clamped shut because the instant it let go, all those years of holding everything in would burst out like water from a fire hose and spew ugliness over anybody around me.

Which meant Lovejoy.

My mouth ripped apart. *Oh, God, help me.*

The torrent broke with a force that scraped my throat and chest. The sounds wrenching out of me were ugly, all right, but they weren't words. I didn't know what they were.

Neither did Lovejoy. "Are you *laughing?*" she said incredulously, pulling me around to face her. My eyes had blurred, but I saw her expression change. "Oh, Bank." She put her arms around me.

I hadn't cried since I was a little kid. Now I held onto Lovejoy and bawled all those years' worth onto her curly brown hair. It would've shaken me apart if Lovejoy hadn't been holding me together. I *was* laughing. And crying. And whatever else you do when life is too sad and weird and wonderful and unbelievably awful to bear.

The whole thing probably didn't last more than a minute, but it could've been an hour. I had no way of telling. No sense of time or place or anything else. I didn't even realize it was over until a muffled voice came from between my arms.

"Has it stopped raining?"

Raining? I opened my eyes and looked down. Lovejoy still clutched my waist, but I'd been holding her, too, with her head wrapped in my arms so only the very top showed. She was right. Her curls looked as wet as if she'd been caught in a storm.

I guess you could say she had.

"Wow, I'm sorry." I let her go.

She stepped back and looked up at me. Her face was rosy and damp, but I couldn't tell if that was from my tears or hers.

At that moment, with wet hair straggling down her forehead, her nose and cheeks red from pressing hard against me, Lovejoy Fox was the most beautiful person I'd ever seen. Maybe later I would feel embarrassed about having bawled all over the girl I most wanted to impress. For now, I just rested in a deep and flowing thankfulness.

Thank you, God.

Because as my mouth had ripped apart, moving to destroy the sweetest gift I'd ever been given, my mind had flashed on Viking Clone. On the pamphlet he'd given me, with the weird little creature and its silent shriek, blowing its world apart. The way I'd wanted to show it to Lovejoy. The words I'd read on the inside pages while I waited for her to come over tonight.

All those things had sliced across my mind barely in time to meet and slam against the speeding ball of rage, knocking it harmlessly away. I'd half-drowned her, but at least I hadn't said anything to hurt her. To hurt us.

I owed Viking Clone more than I could even stand to think about.

Lovejoy pushed her wet hair back and wiped both hands on her jeans. "What was *that* all about?"

"I think it was about, oh, probably about sixteen years."

"What?" Her laugh sounded shaky. "Bank, you're a little wild tonight, aren't you? Should I be worried?"

"Yeah. No. Do you want something to drink?"

"Water, please. Some of that really good water."

It took me a second to catch on. "The bubbly brown stuff?" My grin felt shaky, too. I pointed. "Go on into the family room. Forget the paper. We've got to talk."

First, though, I needed to check on Mom. Even way back in her bedroom, there was no way she could've missed all the commotion I'd made. I headed for the hallway that led to my parents' room. Conflicts with Dad were bad enough with how they affected her. This had been a thousand times more intense.

"Whoa!" Charging past the kitchen doorway, I skidded to a stop and backed up. "I thought you were in your room. I thought you were reading."

"I heard you. You were yelling at that nice girl."

Her forceful tone caught my attention.

"Um, Fighter?"

"You bet." She glared at me. "You stay away from us. I *knew* you weren't safe."

"Everything's fine. I wasn't yelling at her. I was just..." Yeah, right. Try explaining this one.

"Where is she? You hurt her, didn't you? She ran home."

"No, she didn't. She's back in the den. I'm getting her a Dr Pepper. If you don't believe me, go look for yourself."

I turned my back on her and opened the refrigerator. I'd never been that rude to an alter before, but I figured Fighter could take it. She could be pretty rude herself. She stomped off, huffing, and I grinned. Fighter was a brat, but she had spunk. If she could keep Mom from falling apart when things got scary, I was all for it.

When I carried in our drinks, Lovejoy had propped her bad foot up on the coffee table. She held a chocolate chip cookie in her hand and a plate of them on her lap.

I set both glasses on the table. "How'd you get those?"

"Somebody told me where they were." She smiled. "First she asked if you were being mean to me. I said no. Then she asked if I was telling the truth, and she had me do this thing where you hook fingers and swear your ears will shrivel if you're lying."

"Mom came in here?" I hadn't thought she really would.

"Sort of. I mean, it was your mom, but it wasn't." Her smile faded. "I'm glad you told me, or I wouldn't have known what was going on. It *was* a little weird."

"Wow, I'm sorry. I thought she was going back to her room to read. That's what she was doing before, but all that—well, all that noise I made scared her. Then Fighter came out. If anybody gets mad, it really scares my mom."

"Fighter?"

"An alter. She's only five years old. She wouldn't hurt anybody. None of the alters would." I sat beside Lovejoy. "She wanted to protect you from me."

"Good. I need somebody like that." She held up her cookie. "These are the ones from Sunday, aren't they? Is that where you hid them when I asked you to? Under that magazine?" She pointed to the table by Dad's chair.

So that was where the cookies came from. "Good thing you found them before Dad got home," I said. "He wouldn't think it was funny."

"I didn't find them. Fighter told me."

I wondered how Fighter knew. Mom must not have known, or she'd have put the cookies where they belonged. I leaned back and sighed. If tonight didn't scare Lovejoy off, nothing would.

"You're right," I said. "I was a little crazy tonight. But I'm really *not* crazy."

She squeezed my hand. "I know."

"I'll tell you what happened." I turned my fingers to fold around hers. "Or do *you* want to talk first? About what Mandy—"

On the floor beside her foot, Lovejoy's purse burst into song. She took her hand away, and I rescued the plate of cookies as she bent to pull out her phone. The music got louder, and I recognized the theme song from the TV show *Friends*. So the drumrolls and "Hey, boss!" must just be for her mom. Appropriate.

Lovejoy glanced at the screen. "It's just Alex. I don't need to get it."

I checked myself for jealousy. Just a little, maybe, but I didn't want to encourage it. "No, that's okay. Go ahead."

"Alex never talks long. He usually texts."

So did most kids. The only ones who didn't were those of us whose dads had bought the cheapest possible phone plan, then blocked texting to keep their kids from running up extra charges.

Maybe if I got a job, I could get my own plan.

And a laptop. Yeah, right.

I bit into a cookie. Not bad for something that had just spent three days hibernating under *U.S. News and World Report.*

"Hi, Alex. No. No, I don't. Why? Oh, *really?*" Her tone sharpened. "Yeah, of course. Definitely. Bye."

"That was fast," I said.

"Yeah." Frowning, she dropped her phone onto the sofa between us.

"Something wrong?"

She nodded. "This could be really bad." She leaned back and stared up at me. "Tara's missing."

31

Light

I went to tell Mom we were leaving.

She was on her bed, propped against pillows with a blanket over her legs and a book on her lap. Her face looked pale, and I thought I saw someone else peek out for a second. Probably Fighter. I'd have some explaining to do about my tantrum earlier this evening, but now wasn't the time.

"Are you taking Lovejoy home?" She set the book aside. "I'll come and say good-bye."

Wow. If I'd blown up like that a year ago, she would've been hiding in her closet. *Thank you, Dr. Sam.* Maybe there was hope for Tara after all.

I jingled my keys. "Actually, we're going to look for a girl from school. Her parents don't know where she is. We'll drive around and see if we can find her."

"Who?"

"That new girl I told you about. Tara Prentiss."

"Tara Prentiss." Her eyes changed, as if checking inside. "She came here last night."

"Tara was here? At our house?" I thought back. "Was that who rang the doorbell last night?"

She nodded.

"Was she looking for me? Why didn't you call me?"

"Tara wasn't sure if she really wanted to see you. Since I answered the door, she decided to talk to me instead." Her eyelids flickered again. "That's right, she mostly talked to Little Friend. But

I heard it all."

"Little Friend?" What a soppy name. "I haven't heard that one before."

"You don't know her. She's the one who came out that day in the kitchen and was so afraid of you. The day after your birthday, remember?"

"Sure, I remember. What did Tara want?"

"She asked a lot of questions about you. And she said she meets with Dr. Sam, too. That's why her family moved here." She paused. "You know what that means?"

"DID. I figured it out a while ago."

Mom's eyes had darkened with concern. She touched the scar on her throat. "How long has Tara been gone?"

"All day, I guess. Her parents called her friends, and now everybody's calling around. A guy from school just told Lovejoy." I started to move away, then turned back. "I don't suppose you have any idea where she might've gone? You know, since you both—"

"Bank, we have DID," she said. "Not ESP."

"Sorry. I thought it was worth asking." I shrugged. "I'd better go. I don't know when I'll get home."

Mom pushed the blanket back and swung her feet to the floor. "Tara did talk about the school. She told me she wasn't supposed to go back there. But she said she needed to make things right for you."

"She wouldn't be there now. Nobody's there. The buildings would all be locked." I thought about the smooth, dark playing fields, broken by areas of tall grass and bushes. "Do *you* think she'd go there? Maybe out on the school grounds?"

"I don't know. She might. If she's trying to do something she's not supposed to, she'll be scared and confused. Some of the ones inside will want to hide."

Mom went with me to the front of the house. Lovejoy stood by the door with her duffel coat on, phone to her ear.

"Yeah, we're going to look, too," she was saying. "We're

just about to leave. Let me know if you hear anything." She glanced up.

"Tell them to check at the school," I said. "Outdoors, at least. Mom thinks she might be there."

"Bank says try the school grounds. I don't know, but you could look. Okay. Bye." She tucked the phone into her coat pocket.

Mom rummaged in the upper shelf of the closet and emerged with her hands full of gloves and knitted caps. "You might need these. Please be careful." Her eyes looked scared, but it was still Meredith. "I'm praying for her."

It *was* cold. When we got in the car, I pulled my gloves and cap on right away. If Tara hadn't found an indoor hiding place, she'd be freezing.

"Your heater's not very good, is it? I remember that." Lovejoy tucked her curls under a cap and sorted through the gloves for a matching pair. "Look, your mom gave us extras. For Tara, you think?"

"Probably." I started the engine. "Any ideas? You know her a lot better than I do."

"Not really. We just went as a group, to places like Pizza Hut and Starbucks. People have already looked there." She was silent, frowning. "I guess we could try the school."

As I pulled away from the curb, a blanket of unreality settled over me. It felt like that slow urgency you get in a dream, when some horrible disaster is about to happen and you can't stop it. You run because you have to, but you know it won't do any good.

I glanced at Lovejoy as the streetlight flashed across her face. She sat still, staring straight ahead. She didn't seem real either.

We didn't talk at all until we got to the school. The windows were dark, but dots of light bobbed around the grounds. Flashlights. Either whoever Lovejoy had been on the phone with took her suggestion, or other people had already thought of looking here.

"Maybe you should stay in the car," I said. "You might hurt your ankle again, walking around out there. The ground's rough."

"I'm not staying in the car. I'll go slow, but I'm not just sitting here." She opened the door and got out, stuffing the extra hat and gloves into her pockets. "We should've brought flashlights."

"There's one in the glove compartment. And I have mine here." I patted my coat pocket. That's one good thing about having a dad who's an engineer. You never go anywhere without the right equipment.

The sense of unreality stayed with me as we pushed our way through the darkness, our moving ovals of light transforming the familiar grounds into a different planet. Our cold breath fogged the air around our faces, and our feet crunched on short, dry grass and swished through tall, weedy stalks. We stayed together and mostly held hands. I kept quiet, but Lovejoy called Tara's name. Her voice shook with cold, but she didn't complain.

Sometimes it felt as if we'd walked for hours. Then it would seem we'd driven up just five minutes ago.

Maybe I was dissociating. Maybe life looked like this all the time for Mom. And Tara.

Around us, other lights came and went. Kids like us, with no organization to the search, so we probably covered some areas a dozen times and completely missed others.

"It's like fairies," Lovejoy said.

"What is?"

"Listen." She pulled on my arm, and we stopped. "It's just people's phones, but it's like the lights and sounds go together. Like a field of high-tech fairies."

She was right. As we searched, I'd heard different rings, mostly music, cut short as people answered their phones and said a few words before hanging up. If mine went off, we would hear chipmunks singing "Rudolph the Red-Nosed Reindeer," since I still hadn't gotten around to changing it. Not exactly fairylike, but appropriate. Every nose out here must be as red as Rudolph's.

I rubbed my nose with my gloved hand, then pulled out my phone and checked the time. We'd been here almost half an hour.

"Let's go to the car." I stuck the phone back in my pocket. "You can rest your leg awhile, and we can warm up and see if—"

We both turned to stare into the darkness.

"What was that?" Lovejoy's shaky voice didn't sound as if it belonged to her. She gripped my hand. "That was creepy."

"It's Tara."

She shook her head. "No way. That wasn't even *human*."

"Lovejoy." I tried to sound reassuring, but my voice came out unsteady, too. The hair on my scalp and arms prickled, and the flashlight beam wobbled on the ground in front of me. *Come on, manly-man.* "Do you remember me telling you about that time in the parking lot, after the game?"

"When you chased Tara, and I fell down?"

"I didn't *chase* her. Anyway, remember I told you about those weird noises she was making?"

"Oh, yeah. Wow. No wonder it creeped you out." She sucked in a deep breath. "Okay, you're right. It's got to be Tara." Her grip on my fingers tightened. "Wow. No more scary movies for me."

I aimed my flashlight farther out. "Could you tell where it came from?"

"This way, I think." Her light cut to the right, toward the tennis courts. Clutching my hand, she started forward.

With no more sounds to go by, ten minutes later we were still looking, walking in circles. The search seemed as hopeless as ever.

"Wait a second. I have an idea." Lovejoy dropped my hand and fumbled in her pocket. "I'm going to call Tara's cell phone."

I opened my mouth, but she cut me off. "I know that's the first thing everybody did, but I bet nobody's done it for a while. Unless she turned her phone off, even if it's on silent, at least it'll light up. Cut your flashlight, Bank."

Our lights clicked off at the same moment. We stood in darkness except for the small glowing screen of Lovejoy's phone. As she held it to her ear, both of us turned slow circles, staring. But if Tara even had hers with her, it was probably inside her purse or a

190

pocket, and we'd never—

"There!" She pointed.

In the tall grass where Max had searched for a tennis ball a lifetime or two ago, a faint light glowed. Lovejoy got there first, but I was right behind.

Deep in the tangle of rough vegetation, Tara lay curled with one arm extended, the phone resting on her open palm. My sense of unreality deepened. I'd wanted so much to see what was now in front of me, I must be imagining it. Then Lovejoy went down on her knees beside Tara. It was real.

"She's so *cold*." Her fingertips pressed against the outstretched wrist. "But she's alive."

From years with my mom, I knew to be quiet and do nothing that might scare Tara. No telling how close to the edge she might be. Crouching behind Lovejoy, I muttered into her ear. "Stay with her. I'll go tell somebody."

Tara opened her eyes and whimpered.

"It's okay." Lovejoy stroked the leather sleeve and rested her hand on Tara's. "You're okay."

"Here." I pulled off my coat and gave it to Lovejoy. "Tell her it's warm and will keep her safe. Then put it over her. Just keep telling her she's safe."

Lovejoy nodded.

I cut across to the closest moving light and asked the guy holding it if he knew Tara's home phone number.

"No," he said. "Why?"

"Keep your voice down, okay? We just found her."

The beam of his flashlight jerked, but he kept his mouth shut.

"Here's what you need to do." I pointed toward another nearby light. "Go find the next person, and do the same thing I just did. We've got to be quiet so we don't scare her. Keep doing that until you find somebody who knows how to get hold of her parents."

"Okay."

As he started away, I grabbed his arm. "Everybody needs to

191

go back to the parking lot so the only light out here is by Tara. That way they can find us. Lovejoy Fox is with her now, and I'm going back there. We'll keep our lights on."

"Okay. Where is she?"

I recognized him now from Spanish class, a quiet guy named Justin. "She's in that tall grass just west of the tennis courts. How about if you're the one who talks to her parents? I don't know what they'll want to do, because I'm not sure she can walk. I don't know if they've already called the police, or if they'll want an ambulance. You need to talk to them first, so you don't want anyone here calling 911 or anything like that. We sure don't want any sirens."

"I'll take care of it."

As I headed back to Lovejoy and Tara, Justin's light moved steadily toward the one I'd pointed at. Good thing he'd been the closest person. My instructions had sounded confusing even to me, but I had a feeling he'd do things right.

We waited by Tara, who was quiet now and seemed to be sleeping. Lovejoy had put the extra gloves and cap on her. Without my coat, I was shaking with cold. For the second time this evening, Lovejoy wrapped her arms around me, holding me tightly.

We watched the wandering lights stop, one by one, and move toward the parking lot. Finally, everything around us hung dark and silent except the small world of our two lights.

32

Escalation

By the time Lovejoy and I left the school, it felt like we'd been there half the night. I couldn't believe it when I looked at my phone. Barely nine-thirty.

Things had happened quickly once we found Tara. The third guy Justin talked to knew Tara's home phone. Her mom answered on the first ring and called her dad, who was driving around looking for her. They came to the school right away. Justin led them to us, and Tara's dad scooped her up and carried her across the fields to their car as if she was a little girl. The look on his face would rip your heart.

Walking beside me, Lovejoy didn't make a sound. A flash of headlights from the parking lot caught lines of tears sparkling down both cheeks.

I tightened my grip on her gloved hand. "Do you want to go home?"

"We still need to talk. I have to be home by ten, but maybe you could stay for a while."

It felt even colder inside the car than out. Probably a good thing, because as soon as I sat down, exhaustion dragged at me as if the earth's gravity had just doubled. All I wanted to do was lie down and sleep. If the car had been warm, I would have.

Poking the key at the ignition, I yawned. "I think I'm too tired, Lovejoy. I never thought I'd say no to a chance to be with you, but I just want to sleep. For at least a week." The key finally slid in, and I started the engine.

"Not surprising. You're probably on emotional burnout." Her voice sounded as flat as I felt. "A lot's happened."

"No joke."

Tucking the flashlight into my glove compartment, she found an old Sonic napkin. She wiped her eyes and blew her nose. "If you just want to take me to your house, I can call Mom to come get me. That way you could go on to bed."

"No, that's okay. I'll drive you home."

We rode a couple of blocks in silence. Lovejoy sighed. "There *is* something you need to know, Bank. I'm just not sure if you have to know it tonight."

I didn't like the sound of that. But whatever it was, we might as well get it over with. "Go ahead."

"Are you sure? I know you're really ti—" She shrieked as the car shuddered, lurched forward, and died. "I'm sorry," she said instantly. "I hate it when girls scream about nothing."

I shifted into park and turned the key. No life. Tried again. Nothing. Seeing headlights in my mirror, I jabbed the button for the emergency flashers. Getting rear-ended *would* be something to scream about.

"Oh, great." I tried the key again. "This is just great."

"Are we out of gas?"

"No way." Even as I said it, I got a sick feeling.

"It's just, you said something yesterday about being low. I wondered if you'd filled up since then."

"I didn't." I slumped back against the seat. "You're right."

And so are you, Dad. He always said I would someday regret not filling up until the gas gauge showed almost empty.

I sighed. "You'd better call your mom and tell her we'll be late." Not exactly the way to keep Lovejoy's mom on my team.

The headlights behind us belonged to a couple of guys who'd been helping look for Tara. I recognized them as North High conheads, which made me a little nervous. But they were great. They helped me push the Prizm over to the curb. Then, using a piece of

194

hose from their trunk, they siphoned enough gas out of their car and into mine to get us to the closest gas station.

They'd obviously done this before. I had a feeling it usually went the other way, from somebody else's gas tank into theirs. But I wasn't about to ask.

As they stashed the hose back into their trunk, a familiar black Subaru pulled over in front of the Prizm.

Lovejoy looked apologetic. "I didn't know how long we'd be. Mom said she'd rather come get me."

Any other time, I would have resented her mom's interference. Not tonight. All I wanted was to fall into bed and drown in sleep. But before that could happen, I still had to find a gas station, fuel up, drive home, and climb a thousand steps up to my room. If I had to take Lovejoy home, too, I'd probably wind up sleeping in her driveway.

I walked to the Subaru with her and apologized to her mom. Mrs. Fox acted a lot nicer about it than I'd expected.

"Oh, I've done way more than my share of running out of gas," she said. "To tell the truth, I did it just last week."

I tried to laugh, but I was so tired it came out more like a grunt.

"Are you safe to drive home?" Lovejoy asked as I walked her around to the Subaru's passenger side.

"I'm safe. I'm always safe."

She didn't look convinced. "Why don't I have Mom take me to school tomorrow? At least that'll give you extra sleep in the morning."

I wanted to say no, but sleep just sounded too good. "Okay. Lovejoy, you're great."

She pulled my head down and kissed me. Then she stepped back. "That's just to keep you awake until you get home." Her curly smile flashed in the streetlight. "Don't get used to it."

Already, after just two days of taking Lovejoy to school, it seemed wrong going by myself. Empty. I wished I hadn't agreed to that, even though I'd enjoyed those extra twenty minutes under the covers. When I pulled into the school parking lot, I called her cell phone.

"Hi, Bank," came her sleepy voice. "I'm on my way."

I smiled. Definitely not a morning person. "I'll wait for you inside the front door."

"Better not. We just left the house, so I'm barely going to make it. I'll have to go straight to class."

"Lunch in the art room?"

"Yeah, but I'll have to buy something today. I didn't bring a lunch." In the background, I heard her mom say something about breakfast. "So meet me in the cafeteria first, okay?"

"Sure." At least this time she wouldn't have a crutch to swing at me.

Tara made major news this morning. I didn't. Big relief.

Some kids knew about Lovejoy and me finding her, but most thought Justin had. People knew she'd been somewhere on the school grounds, and from there, the rumors went wild. I heard she'd been rescued from the trunk of a car in the parking lot, found locked in the janitor's closet, and caught breaking into the principal's office to steal her own records so nobody could see what was in them.

Whenever anybody asked me, I said Tara had been over by the playing fields. I hoped that made it sound like she'd just been out walking or something normal like that. Not many people asked me about it, though, and my morning went pretty much as usual.

I looked for Lovejoy as I went to third-hour math, but she wasn't in sight. That would have to wait for lunchtime.

After class, Janessa, the girl I'd helped before, had a question about the homework Mrs. Adams had just dumped on us. That made me late getting to the cafeteria. When I walked in, I saw Lovejoy off to the far right, in line at the salad bar.

I also saw sheets of paper being handed around, spreading from person to person. Just like last Friday's email.

No. No way. This time it couldn't be about me.

As I watched, somebody handed one to Lovejoy. She'd just picked up a bowl of salad, but she took the paper with her other hand and glanced at it. Her expression changed. She swung around to face the doorway where I stood. I heard the bowl hit the floor and roll.

That was when I realized that instead of the usual deafening roar of lunchtime in the cafeteria, nobody was talking. Everybody was reading that paper.

Then the muttering started.

"Bank Jonsson." The hiss of the last syllable repeated throughout the room. And, "Look, there he is. That's him. That's Bank Jonsson." The sound ballooned. Voices came from every direction, like being in a gigantic echo chamber. Everywhere, kids gawked and pointed at me.

This *was* about me. What now?

What I wanted to do, of course, was disappear. Back away, like Trevor did when he was accused of cheating two years ago. Run and hide, like Tara. Go deep inside, like my mom.

Maybe it was seeing Lovejoy's stricken face, with all the curl and sparkle drained away, but what I did was step forward.

"What?" I shouted. "What am I supposed to've done now?"

The room shrank into silence again.

Somebody touched my arm and handed me a paper. Another printed-out email. Just like before. At first, my brain seemed disconnected from my eyes, and the words didn't make sense. When they did, they were worse than I could've imagined. If Rob had done this one, too, somehow he'd found out everything I most wanted to hide.

Bank Jonsson was born in an insane asylum.

There it stood, for everybody to see. Right at the top of the page. Part of me stopped there, unbelieving, while the rest of me kept reading. Like in the first email, truth mixed with lies in everything I read.

My mom was crazy, it said, and I'd spent my first year of life in an institution for the criminally insane. Now I was under a psychiatrist's care, too. Like my mom.

As for Tara, she was so traumatized she couldn't talk. But last night when her parents got her home, they saw words written in ink on her wrist. *Bank did it.*

I was the one who knew where to find her. How could I know, unless I'd left her there in the first place? I'd attacked her, dumped her, then played hero by pretending to search for and find her. I'd thought she was dead and couldn't tell anybody who did it. If Lovejoy hadn't been with me when I "found" her, Tara probably *would* be dead.

While I read, the muttering started again.

I couldn't look up. I knew everybody was staring at me. Everybody hated me. This went way beyond giant cooked noodle. This felt more like the volleyball game when the ugly excitement first started to move in, when kids I'd known for years turned against me. *Lord of the Flies.* Ralph, Simon, Piggy…

This email would finish me.

But only if I let it.

My opponent had served, hard and fast. Now I had to return the shot. Crumpling the paper, I threw it straight up, as high as I could.

"I didn't do this." I couldn't believe how my voice carried across the big room, strong and confident like my dad's. "These are *lies.*"

As the ball of paper fell, I stepped forward and smacked it with the palm of my hand. It arched into the middle of the cafeteria and disappeared among the tables.

At a sudden outbreak of voices off to the right, my heart jumped. I turned, half expecting to see a group of kids storming me with knives and forks. Instead, I saw people bending over somebody on the floor. Just like the night in the parking lot.

Lovejoy?

I started forward, but too many people blocked the way. Looking wildly around, I saw the teacher on cafeteria duty heading that direction.

"No wonder she passed out," somebody yelled. "She just found out who you really are."

Like everybody else, I turned to look.

Rob.

"I used to hang out with this guy," he said loudly. "But when I found out—"

"You shut up!"

Heads turned again. Mandy had been crouching beside Lovejoy. Now she stood and pointed at Rob. Small but upright, she looked like an avenging angel in sweatshirt and jeans.

"You're a liar!" she shouted. "You're just jealous, because Bank's the kind of guy you'll *never* be. You want people to think you're so great. But once they get to know you, they see what you're really like. And now he's going to be a big tennis star, and you can't stand—"

Rob's voice tangled with hers and took over. "I just want people to *know*. What about Tara? How about what she wrote? *Bank did it.*"

"I don't believe it!" A high voice beside me piped into the silence.

Heads turned toward Janessa, the math-challenged girl I'd helped. She looked terrified but stood straight. "I don't believe it," she said again. "Bank Jonsson's not like that."

"That's right. He's the only decent guy in this school."

Everybody swung around again, craning to see who'd spoken this time. I stared, too. I didn't even know this girl. Unless—was she

199

the one those guys bullied the other day before I ran them off? That could explain why she didn't think much of the male population here.

Before I could tell for sure, a scrawny little guy spoke up. And then it was like a tennis match, with players scattered all over the cafeteria and spectators trying to keep up with the action.

Then Kevin stood.

"I just want everybody to know," he drawled. "Bank's a *dude*."

Somebody laughed. Someone else yelled, "You tell 'em, Kev!" The sound of laughter grew, expanding, spreading through the cafeteria even faster than the ugliness had. I could literally feel the atmosphere changing. Lightening up. Rising. Everywhere, people batted crumpled paper balls in high, soaring arcs.

Finally, I was free to go to Lovejoy.

33

Winner

"Stop worrying, Bank. It's just low blood sugar. Hypoglycemia."

Lovejoy lay propped on the vinyl sofa in the school nurse's office, her sweat-damp hair drying on her forehead, a chocolate milkshake in one hand. I hunched beside her on a hard plastic chair and held her other hand.

The school nurse, Mrs. Anderson, sat at her desk and tapped at the keyboard of her bulky computer. Probably writing up the masses of reports required by anything that might lead to a lawsuit against the school.

Like somebody fainting in the cafeteria and then insisting she was just fine.

"I'm okay now. I really am." Lovejoy gazed at me earnestly. "Usually it doesn't bother me. But if I get excited when I'm low on calories, sometimes I pass out for a second or two. Eating something fixes it right away. Mandy gave me her sandwich, and I have this shake. I'm fine now."

Mrs. Anderson swung around. "Did you have breakfast today?"

"No. I'm sorry, I know that was stupid. I was running late, so I grabbed a granola bar. But then I didn't feel like eating in the car, so I stuck it in my purse and forgot about it. I really thought I *had* eaten it."

Mrs. Anderson looked at me and shook her head. "Half the girls in this school think they have hypoglycemia. This one really does, and does she take care of herself? No. You'd better go on to class, Bank. Lovejoy, I want you to stay a little longer so I can keep an eye on you."

Lovejoy sighed. "I really am okay."

Letting go of her hand, I stood. "Guess I'll see you in biology. I'll take you home then, right?"

"Right."

She did look paler than usual, and I was glad the nurse was being tough with her. So that explained why people kept telling her to eat. I remembered The Bee saying, "Go ahead and eat, Lovejoy. I don't want you fainting this afternoon." I'd thought The Bee was exaggerating, the way people do, but she'd meant it literally.

Trevor must've known, too. Why didn't I? Lovejoy should've told me so I could look out for her.

Here I went again, trying to take care of everybody. I grinned. For me, this was actually a positive, having a girlfriend with a health problem. Lovejoy suited me even better than I'd realized.

It was a weird afternoon. In the halls, in every class, people looked at me, but this time with full eye contact and mostly smiling.

"Hey, Bank."

"How you doing, Bank?"

"Way to go, guy."

"Heard about the tennis. You going out for the team?"

I could have done without all that, but it sure made an improvement over what I'd been getting lately. Besides, the attention wouldn't last long. Some new excitement would pop up, and kids would forget. Then I could go back to being me.

After fourth-hour English, Rajid told me Max was furious. At Rob, sure, but mostly at lunchtime detention for making him miss the excitement.

In the hall, Josh Sanderson stopped me to apologize for blacking my eye in volleyball. "Maybe you could tell Coach I said I was sorry," he said hopefully, and I wondered what ongoing and brutal punishment Coach Summers had dumped on him.

In biology, Bambi gave me a stick of gum. "It's my last one.

202

Sugarfree. You deserve it."

When school let out, it was a relief to finally be alone in the car with Lovejoy. "Want to come over?" I asked. "We still need to talk, don't we?"

"More than ever." She dug in her purse. "I'll call Mom, but it shouldn't be a problem."

As we turned the corner to my house, a maroon Volvo pulled out of our driveway and drove off. When we went inside, Mom was hanging up my coat. She also had the hat and gloves Lovejoy had put on Tara the night before.

"That was Tara's mother," Mom said. Her eyes looked serious but happy. "We've been talking. She brought these back, and she asked me to give you this." She held out an envelope.

Settled in the family room with a glass of water—the real thing this time—and the last of the chocolate chip cookies, Lovejoy leaned against me as I ripped into the envelope.

"I won't peek," she said. "But you can read it to me if you want."

"Look all you want. They wrote it to you, too."

With her arm warm against mine and her hair tickling my chin, we read the handwritten note in silence.

Dear Bank and Lovejoy,

Tara's father and I will always be thankful for your sacrifice of time and effort to find our daughter. We can never repay what we owe you.

Bank, Tara told us about the terrible misunderstanding at school. We're so sorry you've suffered because of it. We've given a letter to the North High principal and asked that it be made public. We didn't go into detail about Tara's situation, but we made it clear we consider you a fine young man and in no way to blame.

203

Physically, Tara seems fine. Surprisingly so. Even more surprisingly, she seems emotionally stronger, since she now believes she has a friend who truly understands her and wants to protect her when she needs it. I hope you consider her a friend, too, and will stay involved in her life. If not, we certainly understand, but we hope to get to know you.

Lovejoy, thank you for being a true friend. We hope to see more of you, too. We plan to homeschool Tara until she's stronger, and it will be good for her to be around a few people her own age.

> *With sincere thanks,*
> *Tim and Maxine Prentiss*

Lovejoy sighed. "I'm glad she's okay."

"Yeah." I dropped the letter onto the coffee table.

"And I'm glad they wrote that letter. To the school, I mean. That should take care of anybody who's still not sure about you. *A fine young man.*" She smiled.

"Yeah." After today, I wasn't really worried. It was a nice thing to do, though.

"Are you going to do what they asked?" She picked up a cookie. "Get to know them? Be Tara's friend?"

An odd note in her voice caught my attention. I looked down at her curly head. Since she was looking down, too, I couldn't see her face. But her fingers moved restlessly, crumbling an edge of the cookie she held. Grinning, I watched crumbs drop onto her lap.

Aha. If I read her body language right, Lovejoy had a jealous streak of her own.

I opened my mouth to tease her. Then I stopped. This was one peccadillo it was time to give up—saying stupid things to nice people.

Instead, I said, "Hey, I learned something from Trevor a

couple of days ago."

"Oh? What?"

"In tennis, when you make a shot that's so perfect the other guy can't possibly get to it, it's called a winner. That doesn't mean you win the game. But it's just such a great shot, everybody says, 'Wow, that's a winner.'"

"Um-hm." She looked up now, brown eyes curious, a bit of cookie stuck to her lower lip.

I leaned down to brush it away. "That's you, Lovejoy. I've been trying to find the right word for you, and that's it. You're a winner."

"I like that." Her smile curled. "But what makes you think it answers my question about Tara? Or are you changing the subject?"

"I'd rather talk about you," I said.

Sometimes I'm smarter than I look.

34

Disentangle

Mom came in with another plate of cookies and was horrified to find us eating Sunday's stale leftovers. She carried them off, leaving behind the new batch.

Lovejoy leaned over to look. "Lemon bars?" She chose one and tasted it. "Oh-h-h. If I lived here, I'd weigh a thousand pounds. Good thing you're so tall, Bank. You probably couldn't get fat if you tried."

"Want me to hide the rest?"

"Not today. I need all the sweetening I can get. I'd like to *kill* Rob." She sat up straight. "What are you going to do about him?"

"What would I do?"

I honestly wasn't mad. I didn't know why. Maybe it hadn't really sunk in yet what Rob had tried to do to me.

I shrugged. "Mandy already humiliated him in front of the whole school, and then Kevin pretty much finished him off. Now that letter'll make it official. The school might do something to him, especially because of what happened to you."

"Passing out, you mean? I guess that *was* partly Rob's fault." She made a face. "I can't believe I missed seeing you being such a stud."

No one had ever called me a *stud* before. I liked it. "Yeah, well. I can't believe he did it. And I still don't know why."

"I do. Some of it, anyway. Mandy told me."

Part of me wanted to just forget the whole mess. After all, what good would talking about it do? I leaned my head back and closed my eyes. Viking Clone would probably call this avoidance. Something unhealthy-sounding like that. He'd say avoidance was related to suppressing anger and therefore a bad idea. Besides—

Lovejoy poked me. "Bank, you're not going to sleep, are you?"

Besides, it was obvious Lovejoy was determined to talk about this.

"Okay." I opened my eyes. "I'm listening."

"Well, I hope so. Because this is about you." She picked up her glass. "So, anyway, Mandy said things were good with her and Rob until a couple of weeks ago. That's when Trevor told them about the tennis. He said you have the potential to be the best player he's ever seen."

"No way," I mumbled.

"Rob just couldn't let go of it. He kept making these digs about you. Then you and I got together, and Mandy said something about being friends again so we could all hang out. Rob got so mad it scared her. He said you thought you were so great now because of the tennis, but you're just a nobody who needs something like that to feel good about yourself."

That stung. "Why would Rob say that?"

"Because *he* doesn't feel good about himself. He's insecure."

"Rob? He's got to be the most secure guy I know. I've never seen him *not* confident about anything." I sat up straight. "I've been at his house a lot, and his family's great. His parents never put him down or anything."

More than once, I'd wished I could trade places with Rob. His dad treated him way better than mine did me. Actually, his dad treated *me* better than mine did.

"It's a great family," I said again. "Everybody likes his brother. Mac's funny, and he's super-smart. He was senior class president last year."

"I know. *And* Homecoming King, *and* valedictorian. Not to mention editor of the school newspaper." Lovejoy reached for another lemon bar. "I'll bet that's part of the problem. Rob can't measure up."

Lovejoy the shrink. I shook my head. "I don't know."

"Just think about it, Bank. Who does Rob hang out with?"

"Kevin." I thought of the scene in the cafeteria. "At least, he used to."

"Right. Kevin makes him feel good about himself, because Kevin's so clueless. Compared to him, Rob looks like a genius."

"What about Jeff? Jeff's great. Rob hung out with him, too."

"You and Jeff are both so quiet and nice." She set down her cookie and took my hand. "Rob could always be the big leader, bossing all of you around. He tried to make you feel stupid, didn't he? Told you what was going on and made you feel like you didn't know anything."

"Yeah, but that's just Rob. It didn't bother me."

"Well, it bothered Mandy. She finally told her mom about it, and her mom said Rob reminds her of a guy she works with. As long as he's in charge, things are okay. But if somebody else starts looking good, he can't stand it."

"She thinks Rob's like that?"

Lovejoy nodded. "At first, Mandy thought it was her fault Rob was off you. So she kept telling him she'd been wrong and what a terrific guy you were. That's when things really got bad. I guess he thought she was comparing him to you, and he didn't measure up."

I plucked my copy of the second email off the coffee table. "Remember how you said everything in that first email was partly true? This one's the same way. All that about my mom and me being crazy."

"You're *not* crazy." Lovejoy sounded fierce.

"Yeah, but you know what I mean. Part truth, part lie. Mom has DID, which isn't exactly normal. And we both go to see a shrink every week." I held up the paper and pointed. "But this thing about Tara writing *Bank did it*. If it's like the rest, there should be some truth in it. Do you know what that's about?"

"That's what I started to tell you last night. Then your car ran out of gas, and Mom came to get me. We never had time to talk."

My phone rang inside my jeans pocket. Dropping my hand, Lovejoy made an incredulous face. "Rudolph the Red-Nosed—"

"I know, I know. I need to change it." I pulled out my phone. "It's Dad." I flipped it open. "Hey."

"Bank. It's Dad."

"Oh, really?" I grinned. Maybe someday he would remember I still had caller ID. "How's the trip going? Where are you?"

"About twenty minutes away. Are you home?"

"Yup."

"Great. I'll see you then. Let your mother know, all right?" He broke the connection.

"Yeah, right. Love you, too." I closed my phone with a snap. Lovejoy looked sharply at me, but I pretended not to notice. "So, are you up for meeting my dad tonight?"

She nodded.

"You sure? Okay, well, I'll be right back." I stood. "I've got to give Mom a heads-up that he's almost here."

"Why didn't he call her?"

"Free minutes. She doesn't have a cell phone. Doesn't want one. He could call her on the home phone, but this way he saves— what, a whole thirty seconds?" I shrugged. "Be right back."

I gave Mom the message and left her in a flurry of activity, getting ready for the return of the Viking king. Duty done, I dropped onto the sofa beside Lovejoy and picked up the email again.

"So, anyway. This thing about Tara writing on her wrist."

Lovejoy plucked the paper out of my hand. "Okay, now listen. Last night when I was putting the gloves on Tara, I saw something on her wrist. I thought maybe she'd cut herself, but then I saw it was just ink. Words."

She looked up at me. "*Bank did it*. That *is* what it said, and it scared me. Not because I thought you actually did anything wrong, but because it sounded like she was accusing you. I thought it would

209

cause all kinds of trouble."

"No joke."

"Listen, Bank. I kept thinking about that after I went to bed, picturing it in my mind. And then I realized what Tara really wrote."

Lovejoy pulled a pen out of her purse and flattened the email on the coffee table. At the top of the page, she printed *Bank DID*. Under my name she wrote *It*, left a space, then made a squiggly line. She turned the paper so I could see better.

I studied it. "You mean, you think Tara wrote DID, like Dissociative—"

"Right." She nodded vigorously. "It's all in caps. But if you didn't know about DID, you'd just think it was the word *did*. Under that, she started to write a sentence. She got the first word, *It*, and a mark like she was starting something else but quit. *It wasn't his fault.* Something like that. See? The first letter of *It* is capitalized. Like the beginning of a sentence."

She ran her finger under each line. "That's exactly how she wrote it."

"Yeah," I said slowly. "I don't think I told you. Tara was here night before last."

"At your house? Tuesday night? You talked to her?"

"Yeah, she came to our house. No, I didn't talk to her. I was upstairs and didn't even know she was here. She talked to Mom."

"About what?"

"I don't know. Mom only told me last night, when I went to tell her we were going out to look for Tara. She told me Tara said something about going to the school to make things right for me. I guess she was going to tell about her DID and that it wasn't anything I did."

I thought about Mom, about how important it had always been to keep her DID a secret. "You know, that would be an unbelievably hard thing for Tara to do. Really brave."

Lovejoy's brown eyes were intent. "She was gone all day. Do you think she came to school in the morning, then got scared and

210

hid?"

"Could be. You'd think somebody would've seen her, though." I shrugged. "But it fits. If she wanted to tell, some of the alters would try to keep her safe, so they'd make her hide. Then she might've started writing it on her arm, but they'd stop her from doing that, too. They had to keep her from telling."

"Why?"

"It's part of the DID system, part of being safe. You don't tell anything big." I frowned. "I wonder how Rob found out about Mom's DID. Jeff knew, but he wouldn't tell."

Beside me, Lovejoy went still. "That's my fault," she said softly. "It's all my fault."

I almost laughed. That was supposed to be my line. *It's all my fault.*

But she was serious. She held her shoulders straight, just like the time in the gym when she admitted the practical joke while everyone else ran away. Including me.

"What do you mean, your fault?"

She smoothed a bent corner of the paper with one finger, rubbing it over and over. "When Mandy told me she'd just found out Rob wrote that first email, we mostly talked about you. Mandy really does think you're terrific, Bank. I wanted her to know there's even more to you than she thought." She looked up. "So I told her about your mom."

"About the DID?"

She nodded.

"And you told her I'd been born in a mental hospital?"

"Yes. I'm so sorry, Bank." No curl to her lips now.

"Lovejoy, that was a *huge* secret. I told you—" I broke off. "She told Rob?"

"She told him last night, after I called to tell her we'd found Tara. I didn't know Rob was at her house when I called. I told her about what Tara wrote on her wrist, and she told Rob. She told him everything."

211

"Why? Why would she do that?"

"I think…well, she was trying to break up with Rob. He kept saying it was our fault that she wanted to, that you and I had been telling her lies about him. That kind of thing. He said, 'You think Bank is so terrific, but you don't know what he really is.'" She tapped the paper. "He already knew about Dr. Kind. I don't know how."

"So Mandy told him the rest?"

She nodded. "To prove she *did* know and liked you anyway. I'm sorry. I shouldn't have done that."

I couldn't believe it. Now the whole school knew.

"That makes me mad," I said slowly.

"I'm so sorry, Bank." Tears slid into her eyes, but I could see her fighting them back. Her hand had curled into a tight ball with the email crumpled inside.

"You know what? That *really* makes me mad." When I reached for her other hand, her fingers felt cold and tense under mine. "But you're a great apologizer, Lovejoy. You don't make excuses. You just do it."

She blinked. "You almost look happy."

"I am. Almost. I'm finally being appropriate."

"What?"

I quoted Viking Clone. "'Expressing anger appropriately is a protection. It's a pressure valve.' So, I'm expressing appropriately." I grinned. "Wow. This is a *lot* better than the way I handled it last night. I must be a fast learner."

35

Perspective

I heard the front door open, and a jumble of voices spilled down the hallway toward us. I looked up. "Dad's home."

"Let's go see him. Welcome him home." Lovejoy jumped up and stumbled. *"Ow."*

"You okay?" I sprang up, too, and grabbed her around the waist as she balanced on her good leg.

"I turned that ankle just a little when we were looking for Tara. I've been trying to be careful, but I keep forgetting."

The voices came closer. I looked up, expecting to see my parents. Instead—

"What're *you* doing here?" I demanded.

"Hey." Jeff grinned. "That's a great way to greet your long-lost buddy."

I almost fell over the coffee table, getting to him. Behind him, fingers linked with his, came a girl with long brown hair and startled eyes.

"This is Rose," Jeff said. "Who's the football?"

Football? Why would he call Lovejoy a *football*? I turned back toward the sofa. No Lovejoy. That was when I realized I'd grabbed her up in my excitement and brought her with me, tucked under my arm. Exactly like a football with waving arms and legs.

Tennis had definitely given me stronger muscles.

"Cripes. I'm sorry." I set her down carefully. "Are you okay?" I couldn't believe it. No wonder Rose looked so shocked. What a great introduction. I hoped Jeff had already warned her about the black eye.

But Lovejoy was laughing, just like the first time we met when I knocked her down in the hall. "He really isn't as weird as he looks," she told Rose.

"Sure he is. Except weirder." Jeff dropped Rose's hand to give me a bear hug. "Great to see you, bro."

I hugged back, hard. I couldn't speak.

"How'd you get here?" Lovejoy was asking. "Don't you all have school?"

"Early spring break." Jeff let go of me and took Rose's hand again. "Way early."

I got my voice back. "Are you serious? It isn't even February yet."

"I emailed you, man. Last Friday. Some train derailed and there was a chemical spill. Our school's in the evacuation zone. Stinky halls, kids going to the hospital—it was pretty exciting, but I think half of them just imagined they felt sick. It sure didn't bother me. Or Rose."

He smiled down at her. "Anyway, they decided to give us early spring break while they detoxed everything. A lot of kids weren't happy, but for us it worked out great."

I'd been half listening, half trying to figure out how I missed that email. Last Friday? A lot had gone on last Friday. I had a dim memory of being in the middle of an email from Jeff when The Bee buzzed into the lab and broke up my lunch date with Lovejoy. Then came the volleyball game….

"Why?" Lovejoy asked. "What's so great about now?"

For the first time, Rose spoke. "Bank's dad."

With those two words, I could see why Jeff fell in love with her voice before he even knew her.

"He heard about the spill," she said, "and called to see if Jeff was okay. Then he said he'd be in Des Moines, only three hundred miles from Minneapolis. He said he'd pick us up and bring us home with him so we could see you. Jeff really misses you, Bank."

"My dad did that?" *Only* three hundred miles. That meant an extra six hundred, round trip, from Des Moines to Minneapolis and back. Which meant an extra ten or eleven hours of driving added onto the trip home. Plus, that would use gas and mileage Dad wouldn't charge to the company, which meant a big bite out of his own pocket.

"We fly back Sunday morning. Rose's parents know these people who…" Jeff flapped his free hand. "Anyway. You don't need to know all that stuff." He grinned. "So, here we are."

Lovejoy gave him her curly smile. "You made that long drive for just two days here?"

"Hey, Bank's worth it." He grinned. "Besides, I need a break from life in the frozen north." He sang, way off-key, "Minneso-o-o-ota, where the blizzards come sweepin' down the plain."

Rose put her hand over his mouth. "Big baby. This has been an easy winter. So far, anyway."

"I'll be right back," I said.

I tracked Dad to my parents' bedroom. Through the closed door, I could hear them talking. I hesitated. Then I knocked.

Dad opened the door. He'd already taken off his shoes, and he looked tired. I heard water running in their bathroom, which meant he planned to soak in the tub and then go straight to bed, his usual post-trip routine. Behind him, Mom waved at me and disappeared into the bathroom with his pajamas.

"Dad." I stopped. I wasn't even sure what I wanted to say.

"So this is the famous eye." He reached his big hand out to my face. His touch surprised me with how good it felt. "Your mother told me what happened."

I'd gotten used to being taller than everybody except Viking Clone, but I still had a couple of inches to go before I'd catch up to my dad. I felt like a little kid as he studied the bruising around my eye. "Um, thanks, Dad. For Jeff and everything."

"Well." He stepped back. "Just don't be too loud. I need to get some sleep."

"We'll be quiet. Maybe we'll go out somewhere."

"Remember, you can't have more than one underage passenger. And this is a school night. Do you have homework?"

My big paper on *Lord of the Flies* was due tomorrow. He must've seen the expression on my face, but he just said, "Have Jeff help you clear your computer out of the dining room. I'll see you in the morning." He shut the door.

"Love you, too," I said quietly. But this time I meant it.

I guess different people show love and loyalty differently.

And that's okay.

I finished my paper after all.

Lovejoy's mom drove Rose home with them that night, which was Lovejoy's idea and way better than having Rose camp out on our lumpy sofa. As soon as they left, Jeff and I went up to my room. He'd brought me a present.

I pulled it out of the bag and read the label. "A can of air?"

He took it from me. "Should be a little plastic straw in there, too. This is to fix one of your pedakilloes. Pecco—"

I fished in the bag and came up with a short, skinny straw. "Peccadilloes?"

"Whatever. I'm sick of hearing you whine about your computer." Grinning, he poked the straw into the nozzle and took aim at my keyboard. The pressure sent crumbs leaping out to scatter across my mouse pad like a miniature sandstorm. "Whoa. You've got to quit eating at your desk, bro. You got a whole restaurant in there."

"And you've got to quit wasting your money." I swiped the crumbs onto the floor. "I could've bought one of those cans myself.

Save your money for a phone, man."

"Let me see yours."

I handed it over. He flipped it open and started punching buttons.

"What're you doing?" I reached for the phone, but Jeff backed away and popped a few more keys before he gave it back.

"What's—hey." The screen was open at his name in my contact list, and it now included a number. "You bought a phone?"

He pulled one out of his pocket and held it up. "Sam just got a new one. He sold me his. It's a dinosaur, but it works."

We stayed up until two in the morning, talking and trying not to laugh too loud. Then Jeff cleared the junk off my extra bed and crashed, and I went to work on my paper.

Maybe it was the clean keyboard, but the words just rolled out. An hour later, I was in bed, too, with tomorrow's—no, today's—assignment safe in my English binder and ready to turn in. I wrote it from Ralph's point of view, how having the other boys attack him like that affected him through his whole life until he died as a very old man.

I had a feeling this semi-fictional approach might not be exactly what Ms. Montoya had in mind, but I was happy with it.

And after I got the whole thing down on paper like that, remembering the volleyball game didn't bother me as much.

Coincidence? Or psychology?

I'd have to ask my shrink.

36

Resolution

I came home charged and chuffed, letting the door bang shut behind me. Trevor's old racquet felt cold and powerful in my hand. Today had been my first time in days to play tennis after school, and it had gone great.

"I'm home!"

My size thirteen Nikes thumped against the hardwood floor as I went into the dining room, automatically ducking my head in the doorway. I slung my book bag across the floor toward the stairs. It smacked against the bottom step, and my Spanish book shot out and landed halfway up the staircase.

"Whoa, Señor Grande. Better watch out for those new muscles." Grinning, I flexed my right bicep. It didn't look much bigger. "Hey, I'm home!" Setting the racquet on the table, I peeled off my jacket and dropped it over the back of a chair. Then I stood still and listened.

Nothing.

Nothing but echoes of the noises I'd just made dying away…and furtive scrabbling sounds from the kitchen.

Definitely not my imagination.

"Okay, manly-man." I shoved sweat-crusted hair off my forehead. "We've been here before. Let's go."

I stopped in the kitchen doorway and looked around. No one in sight. The refrigerator blocked part of the room, so I leaned out to see around it. My eyes slid reluctantly toward the back door.

That was when I saw her.

"Tootsie Pop!" I said. "What're *you* doing here?"

With a snort, Lovejoy's dog backed the length of the leash someone had looped around a chair leg. Then she charged toward me, barking excitedly.

I crouched to pat her. "Good girl. Where's Lovejoy?"

I got up, wiping dog slobber off onto my jeans, and looked out the kitchen window. Three people stood in our back yard, talking animatedly. Mom, Lovejoy, and...

As I craned to look, the third person moved from behind the others.

Tara!

I jerked back from the window. Tootsie Pop yipped and scrambled out of the way. "Sorry," I said. What was Tara doing here? Cautiously, I edged forward.

All three carried sketchbooks. I watched Lovejoy wave her pencil at a tree and then draw some lines. The other two leaned closer, and Mom pointed at Lovejoy's sketchbook and said something. Tara nodded, pulling the collar of her leather jacket up to her ears. Not the best weather for sketching outdoors, but that must be what they were doing.

I backed away from the window. I wasn't sure what was going on—some sort of art class?—but it didn't look as if they needed or wanted me. Scooping up a handful of cookies, I bulged my eyes at Tootsie Pop and headed upstairs to call Jeff.

He finally answered on the fourth ring, sounding grouchy.

"Whoa," I said. "Sounds like I interrupted something. You with Rose?"

"She's at class."

"I didn't think you guys went back until next week."

"Not school. That genealogy stuff. Family trees. She goes to these seminars to learn the latest software and everything." He yawned. "Our flight home went great, thanks for asking. Just an eight-hour delay because of snow, big surprise."

"The frozen north strikes again." I grinned. Jeff always

turned cranky when he got low on sleep. "Hey, did Rose look at that stuff from my dad yet?"

"Your family stuff? Yeah, while we were waiting at the airport. She had it in her carry-on. There's only about ten million Jonssons in the world, but she says your dad keeps amazing records." He yawned again. "She found a few Kinds hanging on the back of your tree."

"Are you serious?"

"Yeah. She said—hey, that's Rose calling. Okay if I get it?"

"Go ahead. I can wait."

Stuffing a cookie in my mouth, I hit speakerphone. I dropped my phone on the bed and wandered over to the window. Late afternoon sun slanted through the tops of the trees, which meant the day was about to get darker and colder. Lovejoy might need a ride home soon.

I looked down. In the side yard below me, the three girls huddled together on our wrought-iron bench, still talking. Just the thought of sitting on that cold metal gave me the willies.

Wait. The three *girls*.

I looked again. Sure enough, Mom—Meredith—definitely wasn't out. The body language had her younger than Lovejoy and Tara. I took a deep breath. Maybe I should go out and make sure everything was okay. Dealing with a giggly little kid in a forty-year-old body could be weird if you weren't used to it.

Tara leaned forward and took Mom's hand.

I stared. It *was* Tara, but the way she carried herself didn't look familiar. Maybe this was the alter who came to our house the other night. I studied Mom again. And maybe that was the alter with the soppy name who talked to Tara's alter that night. Little Something.

"So, anyway," Jeff's voice announced from the bed, "Rose says your shrink might be a sixteenth cousin ten times removed, but nothing closer than that. Too bad, bro. You can't use the we're-related excuse to quit going. Hey, you still there?"

220

"I'm here." I went over and picked up my phone. "No excuse, huh? Well, *that* stinks."

As the last word came out of my mouth, I flashed on telling Lovejoy about Rob and Kevin's jokey comments about rape and pillage. I remembered saying, "I laughed, but I didn't think it was funny." Lovejoy had gazed up at me with big, serious eyes and asked, "Then why did you laugh?"

Did I want an excuse to quit?

No. Actually, I was looking forward to Wednesday. For one thing, Ms. Montoya had already graded my *Lord of the Flies* paper, and I could hardly wait to tell Viking Clone what she'd written. She said I showed "an unusually mature understanding of the effect childhood trauma might have on an adult."

Big surprise, as Jeff would say.

"Viking Clone's okay." I shifted the phone to my other hand and pulled my snack drawer open. "I kind of like talking to him."

"Well, cool. Hey, how's Lovejoy? I like that girl. I don't know what she sees in you, bro, but I'm glad she does."

"She's here. She's downstairs with Mom."

With Mom. I'd forgotten about them. As I turned toward the window, a door banged downstairs and I heard someone running.

"Bank!" Lovejoy's urgency echoed through the house. "Bank, where are you?"

"Coming!" I bellowed. Jeff gave a pained squawk.

I took the stairs three at a time, lost my footing, and thumped down the last few steps on my rear. As I rolled onto the floor, Lovejoy rounded the corner at a limping gallop.

"Don't *run!*" I scrambled to my feet. "Where is she?"

"Outside. I don't know what's going on. They—"

I took off.

Tootsie Pop yelped as I blew through the kitchen and out the back door. The garden at the far end of the yard stretched empty except for stubs of wintry vegetation, but I stopped to stare. Eight years ago, I'd found Mom there, blood smeared over her throat and a knife on the ground by her hand.

"What're you doing? Come *on*, Bank." Lovejoy grabbed my hand. "This way."

When we reached the corner of the house, I slowed, pulling Lovejoy back. I could see Mom and Tara on the wrought-iron bench. Intent on what they were doing, they didn't see us.

Mom sat very still, her arm extended, while Tara bent over it. Tara's hand was moving, doing something to Mom's wrist. A ray of the setting sun blinked over her shoulder and glinted on her clenched fingers.

"Is that a *knife*?" Lovejoy whispered.

I jerked forward, then slowed. The last thing they needed was for us to go charging at them.

They both looked up as we approached. Tara pulled back, and Mom covered her wrist with her other hand.

"Bank," Mom said uncertainly. I wasn't sure it was Meredith until she spoke again. "When did you get home?"

I stopped a few yards away, aware of Lovejoy still gripping my hand. I tried to keep my voice steady and quiet. "What's going on?"

"We made an agreement," Mom said. She looked at Tara.

Suicide pact. I felt sick.

A chill breeze lifted Tara's hair and spread it across her cheek. She pushed the dark strands back, then thrust her hand toward us. I tensed, ready to act, but the hand was empty. No knife. What was Tara doing? Her sea-green eyes looked darker with the setting sun behind her, and I couldn't read her expression.

"Oh." Lovejoy moved forward, pulling me with her. She plucked something from Tara's lap and held it up. A shiny metal pen. Then she dropped my hand to cradle the wrist Tara still held out. "Look," she said softly.

I half expected to see *Bank DID It* scrawled on Tara's smooth arm. Instead, the inked letters read *Penny*.

Mom said, "That's someone inside Tara. And now she's

gone inside for good." She held out her own wrist, and I leaned down to see what Tara had written there.

Fighter.

Things were starting to make sense. "Fighter went in? Integrated?"

Mom nodded. "I told you I didn't know why integration was going so slowly. Remember? I told you everybody seemed to be waiting for something."

"Sure, I remember. The time Fighter burned the cookies."

"That's right. I think this might be what they were waiting for. Anyway, Tara and I are going to try. One at a time each, we're going to integrate. Together." She smiled. "Fighter wanted to be first."

Fine with me.

Tara finally spoke. "None of us wanted to go first." The supermodel was out again, southern twang and all. "But Penny said she would. She said she was supposed to, because of her special sign."

She pronounced the last word "sahn." Southern. It took me a moment to get it.

"Her sign?" I asked.

Tara reached into her jacket pocket. She brought out a penny and held it up to catch the last of the setting sun. "This showed up from nowhere, in our pocket."

Mom said, "Sometimes God uses odd messengers."

She watched me as she spoke, as if she knew I'd been the odd messenger this time. I didn't see how she could. But I wouldn't put it past her.

"It's still scary." Tara pulled the cuff of her jacket down to cover her wrist. "But we think it's going to be okay."

A small voice spoke from my hand. "Wow, life never used to be this exciting. I moved away at the wrong time."

Jeff. I was still clutching my phone.

"Sorry. Fill you in later," I said and hung up.

"It's getting dark." Mom reached for her sketchbook. "Let's go in. Would you girls like to stay for dinner? Bank's dad won't be here. He has a meeting."

As we headed for the house, Mom and Tara talked about how surprised Dr. Sam would be.

No joke. Team integration. That had to be a first.

Lovejoy and I trailed behind, limping in unison. I surreptitiously rubbed my rear end. At least any bruises from crashing down the stairs would be less public than the black eye.

"Bank." Lovejoy moved closer. "I sort of understand what happened. But not really."

"Want to talk later? I could drive you home after dinner."

"Sure. I could use some pontificating. And maybe a peccadillo or two. Let me call Mom." She pulled her phone out of her pocket. "Do you remember what Rose said when your mom asked her about genealogy? About why she likes doing people's family trees?"

"No. What?"

"Rose said, 'Every part of you is important. Your past is a big part of your present.' Then your mom said, 'And it's all part of who you're going to be.'" Lovejoy's smile curled. "I *like* that."

I took her hand. Her warm, rough fingers closed around mine.

And it's all part of who you're going to be.

Coming Soon

I Didn't See You

Freshman Raye Blackwood likes her life just the way it is. Then the social ladder at high school turns upside down, taking her with it.

Goose Eggs

Fifteen-year-old Teller knows all about Goose Eggs and the fourteen people who've always lived there. After all, she's one of them. But life is about to prove her wrong…and then some.

About the Author

Jill Case Brown lives in Colorado with her husband, David, and whoever happens to be staying with them at the time.

Reach her at:
www.jillcasebrownwriting.wordpress.com
jillcbrown54.jb@gmail.com

62187999R00141

Made in the USA
Lexington, KY
01 April 2017